JILL SANDERS

· THE LUCKY SERIES ·

Sweet✦Resolve

ALSO BY JILL SANDERS

The Pride Series

Finding Pride
Discovering Pride
Returning Pride
Lasting Pride
Serving Pride
Red Hot Christmas
My Sweet Valentine
Return To Me
Rescue Me

The Secret Series

Secret Seduction
Secret Pleasure
Secret Guardian
Secret Passions
Secret Identity
Secret Sauce

The Lucky Series

Unlucky In Love
Sweet Resolve

The West Series

Loving Lauren
Taming Alex
Holding Haley
Missy's Moment
Breaking Travis
Roping Ryan
Wild Bride
Corey's Catch

The Grayton Series

Last Resort
Someday Beach
Rip Current
In Too Deep
Swept Away

JILL SANDERS

· THE LUCKY SERIES ·

Sweet ☘ Resolve

Montlake
Romance

Published by Montlake Romance, Seattle

www.apub.com

Amazon, the Amazon logo, and Montlake Romance are trademarks of Amazon.com, Inc., or its affiliates.

ISBN-13: 9781503935082
ISBN-10: 1503935086

Cover design by Shasti O'Leari Soudant

Printed in the United States of America

*To my sisters, who have and always
will be my best friends.*

PROLOGUE

Amelia rushed through her front door, almost knocking over her little brother, Joel. Instead, she ended up falling backward and landing on her butt, hard. The pain shot up her back, causing the tears that had been in her eyes to flood down her cheeks. After quickly yelling at him to get out of her way, she bolted up the stairs and slammed her bedroom door shut behind her.

She threw her bag across the room and leaned against her door, wincing when she bumped her bruised backside on the door handle. She knew it wasn't her little brother's fault that she'd fallen down. She hadn't seen him because her eyes had been too full of unshed tears. Just the thought of the boy who had caused her the ultimate embarrassment had her vibrating with anger.

Closing her eyes, she flipped around and rested her forehead against her bedroom door as more tears washed down her cheeks. She'd never been so humiliated before. It had been his mission to embarrass her ever since he'd moved in down the street during her kindergarten year.

It wasn't as if her life would have been all peaches and cream even if she weren't being bullied by a boy half her size. She sighed and opened her eyes to look around her room. There were still boxes shoved in the corner and piled high in her closet.

She had been awakened in the middle of the night a few days ago by the sounds of her mother packing up all her things. "Mom, what are you doing?" Amelia had asked groggily.

"Oh, Amy," her mother croaked out her nickname. Her mom had rushed over to her, crying as she tried to explain. But she hadn't made any sense sitting next to Amy, babbling as tears rolled down her face. But then Amy had heard one word she did understand. *Divorce.* Even though she was only eleven, she'd felt much older after her mother told her that she and her father were getting a divorce.

When what was happening finally registered in her sleepy mind, she'd instantly thought of Kristen, her best friend in the whole world. They'd known each other since kindergarten. She couldn't possibly move away from Kristen. Amy had begged and pleaded with her mother that night while the distraught woman had rushed around tossing clothes and items into boxes.

Finally, her father had walked in and taken her mother's arm, and together they had left the room. Her father had glanced back at Amy as she cried on the edge of her bed.

"It's okay, sweetie. Go back to sleep. We'll talk about all this in the morning." Her father's voice had soothed her then.

Less than a month later, her father had moved into a small apartment in downtown Golden, Colorado. Even though her parents still weren't officially divorced, she found it difficult to get over the fear that, at some point, her mother would sweep in and finish packing up her things and they would move far away. Because of this, she'd kept everything in boxes, unsure of what would happen next.

Amy walked over and flung herself on her bed. But as bad as her family life was, it still didn't scratch the surface of what had been done to her on the bus ride home. Her back teeth clenched at the mere thought of him.

He teased her about everything. For the past couple of years it had been her height. Amy was tall for her age—she was taller than most of her girlfriends, which meant that she towered a foot above all the boys in her class also.

She rolled over and hugged her pillow to her belly. Her silent tears slid across the bridge of her nose and fell to her pillowcase.

Kristen would have normally been there to defend her against the bully, but her friend's parents had picked her up early that day for a dentist appointment. Amy wished she'd been the one to go to the dentist instead. She hated this boy more than going to Dr. Stein's office.

By tomorrow morning, everyone in her entire school would know what he'd done to her. Then there would be no stopping the flood of humiliation that was sure to follow her all week long. All of a sudden, moving away didn't seem so bad.

She glanced down at the boxes, then over at the picture of her and Kristen on her nightstand. Shaking her head, she decided that nothing could ever be bad enough for her to move away and give up her best friend. Especially anything Logan Miller could ever do to her.

CHAPTER ONE

Fourteen years later . . .

Amy's heart skipped a beat as she watched the man walk into the conference room. Her presentation had been going smoothly up until that moment. Now, she could only blink and stare at him, as if she'd seen a ghost.

Instead of coming in and finding a seat, he'd leaned against the closed door with his arms crossed over his chest. His suit looked expensive and she could tell that he was comfortable in finer things.

His silver-blue eyes bore into her own. He was easily the tallest man in the room, nearing six-two. His nose was straight, but it was his chin and lips that drew most of her attention. Talk about perfection! How did he get such a good-looking face?

His sandy-colored hair was the only part of him that looked disheveled. But since there was a high-wind advisory in effect for that day in the foothills of Colorado, she guessed that he'd just arrived and the wind had had its way with him. Earlier that day, she had taken a few minutes herself, in the ladies' restroom, to put herself back together after the short walk from her car to the office building of Rocky Mountain Realty, her employer for the last several years.

It had taken several seconds of watching him before her mouth started working again. She'd stood in front of the rather large group of employees with her mouth open, blinking at him, before she'd shaken her head and glanced down at her notes.

As long as she didn't think about the sexy man leaning against the doorway, or what his presence meant, she felt like she could continue with her presentation. However, after looking down at her notes, the words seemed to float on the paper in front of her. It took all her concentration to continue with her presentation on how to properly enter a listing into their new computer system. She'd headed up this project, since she'd been the one to suggest the upgrade to her boss, Gary Bortolo. Gary wasn't only her boss; he had always been a very close friend of her father's.

The year she'd been hired at the agency, rumors had spread that she'd gotten the job due to favors. She knew how to handle gossip, and it had taken her less than a year to start climbing the corporate ladder.

Now, her office was the second largest in the building, and she was credited for single-handedly turning the agency around. This was just the surface of what she had planned for the agency. Especially since she had her eyes on becoming RMR's first partner. If she could persuade Gary to take her on.

The rest of her presentation went smoothly, as long as she didn't look at the man standing near the back. Her mind kept running over the same question: What was he doing here?

Finally, she shut down her laptop, switching off the projector. Gary was the first one to approach her.

"Good job, Amy." He smiled and patted her on the shoulder. "This system should speed us up as well as stop Leah from losing paperwork." He said the latter part in a whisper as he leaned closer. He nodded toward the older woman who was the primary cause of all lost paperwork in the agency. Amy couldn't stop her smile or the laughter that came quickly.

"Only if she doesn't lose her computer mouse again," she whispered back.

He laughed as he looked toward the man who was approaching them. "Aah, just in time for introductions." He reached out and shook the man's hand firmly. "Glad you could make it."

"Almost got blown away." The man chuckled and the sound caused a shiver to run down her spine. She realized her back teeth were clenched and she had to work to purposely release her jaw.

"Amy, this is Logan Miller, one of last year's top, up-and-coming Realtors in Colorado." Gary patted Logan on the shoulder. "Not to mention, he's my sister's kid." Logan smiled, showing off perfect white teeth, which only caused Amy's eyes to narrow. "I'm happy he's finally decided to come work for me." Gary patted him on the back again. "I want the two of you to work closely for the next several months. We have some big projects coming up and we need the extra help."

She nodded and looked down to see Logan's hand stretched out toward her. It took all her willpower to raise her hand and shake his. She tried to pull it away quickly, but he held onto it and smiled a little more at her.

"Nice to meet you, Amy. I'm sure I'm going to enjoy working with you."

She tugged her hand free. "I . . ." She felt her chest grow tight and looked around for an escape only to blurt out, "I need to go to the restroom." Her cheeks heated once the words left her mouth, so she gathered up her laptop quickly. When she turned to leave, she watched as Gary started making his way around the room, introducing her nemesis to the entire workforce at RMR. Her eyes met Logan's as she pushed through the doorway. She thought she saw his smile grow, but didn't linger to make sure.

She rushed back to her office and dumped her computer, then glanced at her clock and wished more than anything that she didn't have another hour before she could clock out. Picking up her cell phone, she texted Kristen and told her she needed to stop by her place after work.

I'll be there. Is everything ok? Kristen texted back.

Just be there. Pls, she responded.

Always! her friend answered.

She felt her eyes sting and took a couple of deep breaths to clear her mind. Why hadn't she known that Logan Miller was Gary's nephew? She knew that Golden was a small town, and after living here her entire life, she knew that almost everyone was related to someone she knew.

She sat down hard in her leather chair. Closing her eyes, she started swiveling her chair around and tried not to think of the possibility that Gary was bringing Logan in to take over the business.

For months now, she'd been thinking that she finally had a shot at persuading Gary to take her on as partner. He'd even given her hints that he was looking for someone to help relieve some of the burden of running the place by himself.

Had he been talking about Logan all along? She opened her eyes and felt her heart sink. Then gasped when she saw Logan standing on the other side of her desk. He had a box of things in his hands and he was smiling at her again.

"Sorry, didn't mean to startle you."

She sat up, making sure to straighten her shoulders. "No, you didn't. How can I help you?"

He glanced around. "Um, it looks like we're roommates for a while."

"What?" She almost jumped out of her chair.

"At least until they find a place for me. Gary told me to park it there." He nodded over to the left corner of her office where a smaller desk sat. She used the spot occasionally, and even had an intern from the local high school who came in once a week and worked there.

She motioned for him to go ahead, then spun around to work on her computer. She tried to keep herself busy for a while. The next time she glanced down at her watch, she almost groaned with frustration. Only five minutes had passed. Glancing at Logan from the corner of her eye, she watched as he set up his corporate-assigned laptop.

"So, what made you choose the Netell system?" His voice almost made her jump.

She turned her chair toward him, her eyebrows shooting up. "It's the best system for what we do."

"Still, it's one of the most expensive out there." It wasn't something she hadn't heard before, or thought of herself, but she still believed in her research.

She shrugged. "It will easily pay for itself within a year."

"We'll see." He turned back to his computer and she felt like throwing something at the back of his head.

Why was he messing with her? Did he think he could just pick up where he'd left off years ago? At this point, he hadn't given her any clue that he knew who she was or remembered her. Had he?

She remembered the day she'd gone to school and found out that he'd moved away. It had been the best day of her junior high life.

Now, he was back and she had no doubt that her life was going to take a turn for the worse. Even if he didn't remember their past, she knew he was trouble. She desperately wished for her friend's advice and mentally counted down the seconds as she pretended to be busy on her computer.

At four thirty sharp, she started collecting her things. Her eyes moved over to where Logan sat with his back toward her as he punched away on his computer. She knew he was faking it, since it was his first day on the job. What could he possibly have to do?

She took a step closer to him so she could get a better look at his screen over his shoulder.

He was working on an email, then she noticed to whom he was sending the long message and she felt her body vibrate with anger.

"Why are you emailing Mr. Kent?"

He glanced over his shoulder at her, his fingers only pausing on his keyboard. "Because his contract was missing the disclosures."

"No. They weren't." She took another step closer to him.

"Yes," he stopped typing and turned toward her, "they were." His lips curled up in a slight smile.

She crossed her arms over her chest. "I hand-delivered them to him on Monday."

"Then you forgot to put a signed copy in his file." He leaned back in the small chair, watching her.

She sighed, knowing exactly where the paperwork had gone astray. "I'll deal with it."

His eyebrows shot up in question.

"Do not send that email. I'll see to getting the paperwork in his file myself." She turned to do just that, but his voice interrupted her.

"If there's deadweight in the agency . . ."

She spun around quickly and stormed over to him. "There isn't. Everyone here pulls his or her own weight."

He waited a moment, then nodded slowly. "Fine. Have it your way."

She looked down at him, then turned toward the door. She stopped with her hand on the handle. Something nagged at the back of her mind. Why was he here? And more importantly, why now?

"What are you doing here?" she asked, not looking back at him.

"Same as you, I suppose."

She turned toward him to question him further, but then he continued. "It's the best move for my career. RMR is a good, solid agency. There's great potential here."

She couldn't have argued that point. Not since she believed it herself. Turning, she opened the door and rushed out to find where Leah had misplaced Mr. Kent's disclosures.

♦ ◆ ♦

"Can you believe it?" Amy almost screamed. Her fingers were deep in her long hair, and for a moment, she felt like pulling it all out.

"Calm down," Kristen said, leaning back on the large sofa. "Take a deep breath and start at the beginning."

Amy closed her eyes, took a deep breath, and then opened them again and started babbling.

Kristen interrupted her halfway through her story. "Okay . . ." She walked over and took her friend by the shoulders. "First off, who's Logan?"

Amy blinked at her a few times. "Logan Miller." She paused, waiting for recognition to cross her friend's eyes. When none came, she continued, "From junior high school." She paused again and still Kristen didn't seem to know whom she meant. "Bully Logan Miller."

She watched Kristen's eyes sharpen. "Logan? From school? Itching-powder Logan?" Amy nodded. "What about him?" Kristen asked.

"He's my new partner."

Kristen coughed and almost choked on air. Amy slapped her on the back several times.

"What?" Kristen finally squeaked out.

"At work. Gary brought him in to be my partner. I'll be working side by side with him for the next several months." Amy dropped her arms and started pacing again. "Several months of that man. Gary better retire and leave that business to me, that's all I'm saying." Amy turned and swung her hands around. "If not . . ." She tried very hard to steady her anger and fears.

Kristen started laughing. "Logan Miller is your new partner?"

Amy's eyes got big. "Hello?" She waved her arms around again. "That's what I've been telling you for the last half hour."

"Oh, that's rich!"

Jill Sanders

Amy stood back as Kristen continued laughing.

"It's not that funny." She frowned down at her friend. "Can you believe the man didn't even recognize me?" At least he'd acted like he hadn't recognized her. Maybe this was just another one of his games.

"Well, yeah!" Kristen nodded. "Look at you. You're hot!" She smiled when Amy glared at her. "I just mean that you've changed so much. Plus, everyone calls you Amy now, not Amelia. And you did change your last name when your parents got divorced. You're Amy Walker now, not Amelia Craig."

"Still, the least he could have done was remember the person he used to torture every waking moment of every miserable day of his youth."

Kristen gasped. "Oh!" She started walking around the room, much as Amy had been doing a few moments ago.

"What?" Amy followed her. "What?" she kept demanding as Kristen repeatedly said, "Oh!"

Amy was a good deal taller than Kristen. With her long stride, she kept having to avoid stepping on the back of Kristen's feet as they walked.

Then Kristen stopped and Amy bumped into her. Kristen turned and grabbed Amy's shoulders.

"How about we use this temporary memory lapse of his to our advantage?"

"What?" Amy asked, looking down at her.

"What would you say to getting even?"

◆ ◆ ◆

A bottle of wine later, they had compiled a list of the top ten infractions Logan was guilty of in their youth. Which didn't help Amy, since she was unsure how she was going to get even with him for any of them.

"Promise me you'll think about it," Kristen said, pacing the rug. "I mean, do you remember the time he sat behind you on the bus and then accidentally sneezed, causing his gum to fly out of his mouth and straight into your hair?" Amy reached back and touched the spot she'd had to cut out.

"Fine, I'll think about it." Amy looked down at the list and frowned. "I'm just not sure there is any way to do any of this to him."

Kristen smiled. "When the time is right, you'll know. Just promise me that if you can, you'll take the chance."

"When did you become so vicious?" Amy asked.

"When I watched a twelve-year-old boy push my best friend into a frozen pond." Kristen returned to the sofa next to Amy.

Amy remembered how Logan had lost his balance on the school hike. "He didn't exactly push me." She could still recall how cold the water was and the flu she'd had because of the dip.

"No, but he didn't help you out of the frozen mess either." Amy watched as Kristen's frown deepened. Amy knew her friend too well to know Kristen wasn't going to let go of this plot for revenge now.

Amy thought about it and finally gave in. "Fine, if the occasion arises, I'll consider doing something in retaliation." She doubted she would have the guts to do anything besides making a list and dreaming about revenge.

Kristen crossed her arms and gave her one of her most stern looks.

"Fine!" Amy threw up her hands. "I'll do it!"

CHAPTER TWO

Logan watched the sexy woman with golden hair walk into her office the next morning. She was taller than most women and her legs looked even longer in the fitted black slacks she was wearing today. He'd enjoyed the view of her legs the day before, too, in the pencil skirt that had hugged her every curve. She looked like she kept in shape and he could tell that she didn't just spend time in the gym, but the outdoors as well. Her skin glowed with a silky tan, accenting the ultra-blonde highlights in her hair and setting off her blue eyes.

As with yesterday's outfit, nothing was out of place. Perfection was the word that flew through his mind.

He'd made sure he'd been at the office an hour early, just so he could do a little more research on her recent past. Of course he'd remembered everything from their childhood, but hadn't hinted to her that he knew who she was. Something told him to keep that knowledge from her. Maybe he had taken cues from her to avoid mentioning their mutual past, or maybe he had just wanted to see how she would react to him first.

He'd been frustrated when all he could find out was that she'd been working for his uncle for almost four years, after interning in the office while she was in college. And in that time, the agency had increased profits almost fivefold.

Not only were profits up, but the business as a whole was gaining a reputation for excellence. Not that RMR had a bad reputation. His uncle had started the business back in the seventies and a few years back, things had started to slow down when the business seemed to fall into a rut. That was, until Amy had joined the firm—then things had started thriving when she'd persuaded his uncle to make a few changes.

Uncle Gary was almost fifteen years older than his sister, Logan's mom, Gina. The siblings had drifted apart as adults, but when Gina gave birth to Logan, her brother had shown interest in his nephew and then in Logan's younger sister, Laura, as well.

His uncle had never married and had no children of his own. Logan's mother had always said that her brother had been married to his business, and after seeing the way the man worked over the past few days, he understood that all too well now.

When Gary had approached Logan a few months ago about joining his business, at first his nephew had been hesitant. Then, after doing some reading about how RMR had taken a turn for the better in the last four years, Logan had been curious to find the reason why.

Everything he'd found had pointed to one person. Amy Walker.

He knew that his uncle was planning on retiring within the next five years; that was certainly an incentive to come on board. But if Logan had to be honest with himself, Amy had been one of the main reasons he'd taken the job. He'd asked his uncle to allow him to work closely with the woman for a while, at least until he had learned how everything ran in the office.

"Morning." He leaned back in the small chair and watched as her eyes heated when she noticed him in the corner.

"Morning," she mumbled and took another sip of her coffee. "You're here early."

"Since I missed half of your presentation yesterday, I'm trying to get familiar with the system."

"Let me know if you need any help." He watched her rush over to her desk and sit down. She looked nervous today, and he knew exactly how to push her further.

"I noticed you have a few meetings today. I hope it's okay if I tag along?"

She glanced up at him. "I suppose you'll need to." He watched her bite her bottom lip and he felt his pulse jump. "I don't even know your history." Her face flushed. "I mean, where you worked before this."

He couldn't stop the smile from bursting onto his lips. "I was at Cherry Creek Realty in Denver for almost four years. I started there shortly after I graduated from CSU."

"Do you still live in the Cherry Creek area?"

"No, I moved back to Golden a few months ago." He knew he should be up front and tell her he recognized her, but he was enjoying his secret too much to stop.

"Being local makes it easier. The commute would have been bad during the winter months."

He smiled. "I hear from my uncle that you do a lot of sales in the mountains." He enjoyed the way she played with a bracelet on her wrist. It was a nervous habit she'd always had.

"Black Hawk has been booming the last few years. Idaho Springs is always busy during the summer months as well." She flipped open her laptop.

"RMR used to only work in Golden."

She glanced up at him. "Yes, it's one of the first changes I made, once I convinced your uncle, that is."

"Sounds like it paid off." He'd seen the numbers himself. It had caused their profits to spike within the first few months.

She nodded, her gray-blue eyes watching him closely. There was something else hidden behind them and he wondered if he'd get a chance to find out what it was.

"I have a nine thirty in Clear Creek Canyon."

"Mind if I ride with you?" he asked, hoping she would agree.

"Fine, I've got a few things to do first. I'll meet you in the lobby at nine." She twisted her bracelet once more.

He turned back to his laptop, hiding his smile of satisfaction. He heard her leave and quickly immersed himself in the files marked Clear Creek Canyon on the shared network drive. There were more than a dozen houses for sale in the area, but he quickly found the file she was working on and familiarized himself with the house and location.

Working in the city for the last few years, he felt unfamiliar with how realty worked in the mountains. It was almost like they were two different animals.

In Cherry Creek, a prominent neighborhood in Denver, it was the square footage of the house that mattered. In the mountains, it appeared that the size of the lot and its location were the most important client concerns.

This particular property had two acres and was sitting on a rather ominous-looking cliff. He bet the view was something to behold, though, and he was actually looking forward to seeing the property firsthand.

By the time he was done reading over the file and looking at all the photos, it was time to meet Amy in the lobby.

He jogged down the stairs and walked into the empty lobby area. Glancing around, he looked down at his watch and frowned. Then he heard a horn and turned toward the glass doors to see her sitting outside in a white Jeep.

It was mid-July in Colorado, and as he stepped out, the warmth of the sun hit him. He loved this time of year in the Rockies. The wind rushed off the foothills, cooling the evenings down for everyone to enjoy.

"I thought we'd drive with the top down," she said as he opened the door.

"Sounds good to me. Nice Jeep." He'd noticed the larger tires and couldn't help but feel a little jealous.

"It comes in handy when the property is at the end of a muddy road." She threw the Jeep into gear and swung out of the parking lot quickly. "Did you get a chance to check out the property?" she asked as they pulled onto Highway 6.

"Yeah, looks like it should have no problem selling."

"You would think so, until you see what it was like before I got my hands on it." She glanced over at him. "They had furniture from the eighties."

"It can be difficult selling a home when buyers can't see past the history of a place." He'd had his share of vintage places to sell.

They drove in silence for a while. He enjoyed the view of the hills as they headed deeper into the high mountains. Clear Creek Canyon was to the left of them. When she turned off the main highway, her Jeep easily started climbing up the side roads.

"Tell me a little about yourself," he said after a while. "I mean, if we're going to be working closely with one another, we might as well get to know each other better." He turned to look at her. She glanced his way and he saw her eyebrows squish together. "Don't you think?"

"I suppose so. You first." She took a turn off the side roads and started up a narrow private road.

"Born and raised in Golden until junior high, although my family moved to a Golden neighborhood with better schools when I was starting kindergarten. Then my folks moved to the Cherry Creek area where I finished school, went to CSU, and started working for CCR." He waited for her to start.

"Married?" She peered at him from the corners of her eyes. He tried to hide his smile as he shook his head.

"Never. Got close a couple of times." Her eyebrows shot up in question. He didn't feel like going through the details now. "Long story." This time when the Jeep turned, he held onto the seat as the tires hit big holes in the dirt road. Dust flew behind them in a big plume.

"Your turn," he said between bounces.

"Pretty much the same as you. Except I didn't move away." She was concentrating on avoiding the bigger holes. The rest of the bouncy trip they sat in silence.

Logan kept his eyes straight ahead, lost in thought until they turned a corner and the house came into view. He whistled. "What a beauty."

She stopped the Jeep in front of a giant four-car garage. "Yeah, I liked it the moment I set eyes on it."

"Makes me wish I had a few million sitting around to snatch it up."

"I don't think I could handle the drive every winter."

"It's not about the drive, it's about that view."

She stepped out of the Jeep and used her side mirror to remove the hat and scarf in which she wrapped her long hair up. By the time she was done, she looked like she'd just stepped out of a salon.

When she turned toward him, he heard a car coming up the long drive and watched as a dark Mercedes SUV rounded the corner.

Over the next hour, Logan observed Amy closely as she worked. By the time the young couple looking at the Clear Creek Canyon property climbed back into their luxury vehicle, he was thoroughly impressed with her. There was no doubt in his mind why RMR was doing as well as it was with her on board.

"Most impressive," he said as they stood on the large deck and watched the dark SUV disappear down the drive.

She turned to him, and for a moment, he could tell that she'd forgotten he'd even been there.

"Thanks." She turned back to the house.

"What a view." He propped his hip on the railing. He felt very comfortable in the nature surrounding them. The air was crisp and clean with hints of pine, and he wished he could bottle it all up and take it back to the city with him.

She stopped, then walked back over to the edge of the deck that overlooked the canyon.

"When I was a girl, my parents owned a place not far from here." She leaned her elbow on the railing.

"What happened to it?"

"They sold it when they divorced." He could hear the sadness in her voice.

He walked over to her and took her hands in his. "I'm sorry."

She jumped a little and frowned at him.

"What?" he asked as her fingers dropped from his.

She blinked a few times, then shook her head and walked into the house without another word.

He stood there for another minute before he walked in the back door to go find her.

"We'd better get back to the office," she said with her back to him. She was putting some paperwork into her small case.

"How many showings can you do in a day?" he asked offhand. "I mean, if every house is thirty minutes away from the office."

She turned to him. "Normally I don't schedule just one showing like this."

He leaned against the counter and waited.

"This is the second time I've shown this couple this house. I'm betting they'll make an offer before the end of the month."

"I'll take that wager," he said under his breath.

She glared over at him. He couldn't help smiling back at her.

"What makes you think they won't?" she asked.

"Oh no. First the wager. It wouldn't be fair to show you all of my cards first."

She thought about it for a moment, then nodded. "Fine, what shall we bet?"

"Dinner," he said smoothly.

Her chin dropped. She recovered quickly and shook her head.

"No?" He leaned up. "Do you have a problem going to dinner with a coworker?"

She nodded slightly.

"Why? Are you married? Seeing someone?" He already knew the answers, thanks to a Q&A session with his uncle that morning.

She hesitated for a split second. "No."

"Good, then it's settled." He felt his heart skip. It was going to be a lot easier getting what he wanted than he thought.

"What do I win?" she asked.

He smiled slowly. "Dinner with me."

She laughed quickly and he realized he enjoyed the sound very much. He also realized it wasn't going to be easy getting her to budge about not wanting to go to dinner with him.

"Fine, if it can't be dinner, how about you get your office back?" he added.

She tilted her head and looked at him. "I'm going to get that back anyway."

"Eventually, but not by the end of the month."

"Fair enough." She held out her hand for him to shake.

◆　◆　◆

Amy was quiet on the drive back down the mountain. Why had she let him sucker her into the bet? Maybe it was the cocky smile on his face?

After all, she knew her buyers. She was positive there was an offer coming soon. Glancing over at him, she wondered what knowledge he had that made him so sure of himself.

The young couple, the Lufts, had shown nothing but eagerness for the house. They had asked all the right questions, already had bank approval, and were sitting on a fortune thanks to a recent inheritance. Besides, she knew something Logan didn't. They were expecting. She knew Logan hadn't picked up on the subtle hints from the couple. Which, in her mind, gave her the upper edge.

Dinner! It was hard to believe that he'd want to spend any time with her, let alone go out to dinner with her. Did he really not know who she was? She wasn't ready for dinner, maybe never would be, which is why she was more comfortable betting on his early departure from her office.

It wouldn't be hard to find out that they'd gone to school together. After all, she had told him she'd been born and raised in Golden, just as he had been.

Maybe he was playing her? She felt her spine grow stiff and thought about her promise to Kristen and the list tucked away in her purse.

As they pulled up to the office building, she remembered a particular item on the list that she could easily get away with and smiled.

"I've got to make a personal run. I hope it's okay if I drop you off here." She nodded toward the side of the building.

"Sure, no problem." He got out quickly, and she felt a wave of excitement rush through her. She clenched her back teeth to keep from making a sound as he exited her Jeep.

Watching him walk up to the side of the building and open the outer doors was the most fun she'd had in a long time. Then she waved at him as he walked right into his first payback.

◆　◆　◆

Logan glanced over his shoulder as the Jeep sped out of the parking lot. He was having a hard time narrowing down exactly what he found appealing about Amy. Maybe it was the sexy way that not a single hair was out of place on her head. She had a body that would stop any man's heart, but there was something else behind those light eyes of hers that caused him to want to dig deeper.

He wanted to see exactly what it would take for her to cut loose. How she would look after a night in his bed. He was so deep in thought, it took him a moment to realize that the inner door wasn't opening right away. He tried the door handle again and this time tugged a little harder. Nothing. Turning back to the outer door, he stopped and stared in amazement. There wasn't a door handle on the inside of the outside door. Running his hands over the smooth surface, he looked around for a keypad or a scanner.

He knew that the building maintained a high level of security, since he'd been given a badge yesterday. But there was no way he was gaining admittance through either door.

He was trapped.

Turning back around, he tried the other door one more time. It didn't even budge. Pulling out his cell phone, he frowned when he noticed he didn't have a signal. Walking around the small space, he tried every angle with his phone. Still no signal.

Tucking his phone back in his pocket, he started pounding on the door. He knew exactly why he was locked in the stairway and thought it was just too good an opportunity to pass up acting like he didn't know what was going on.

CHAPTER
THREE

Amy felt a little relieved when she walked into her office and saw Logan at his desk. She knew that he'd probably spent only a few minutes in the small space before someone rescued him.

But even knowing that it had only been a short time, she'd at least paid him back for locking her in a broom closet in grade school. To this day, she still had problems with confined spaces because of that incident. She still asked herself why she had ever believed him that there was a cat locked in the janitor's closet in the first place.

She smiled when he glanced her way. "Got a call from the Lufts while I was out," she said.

"Oh?" He turned his chair toward her. "Did they make an offer?"

Her smile dropped just a little. "Not yet, but I'm sure it's coming."

His smile grew and he leaned back in the chair as he crossed his arms over his chest. "We'll see about that."

"I have another showing in half an hour." She set a folder down on her desk and started organizing paperwork, removing the file on the

Lufts and adding the two files she would need for her next showings. "Two of them actually, but this time they are in town."

"By the way, I wouldn't use the side entrance anymore. At least not until they have the door fixed."

She glanced up at him, her eyebrows going up in question. She was sure he could see her heart beating from across the room as she waited for his next words.

"I was told the lock is jammed on the inner door. I wouldn't want you to get stuck like I did."

She hated that she couldn't read his thoughts. Was he hinting that he knew she'd sent him into the trap on purpose? He must know.

She nodded, because she didn't think she could contain the lie if she opened her mouth and spoke.

"Now, if you give me the addresses on the listings, I'll do my research."

She sat down behind her desk, making sure to swallow the confession that was on the tip of her tongue.

What had made her think that she could do something like this and get away with it? she asked herself as she rattled off the addresses of the two listings to him.

For the most part, he didn't even look fazed from the whole ordeal. She'd been anxious the entire last half hour thinking of him locked in the small space, and here he was sitting in the office like nothing had even happened.

Maybe that, too, was part of his plan. To throw her off. She wished she was better at games, but she'd never been able to keep a poker face very well.

She'd tried to play an April Fool's trick on Kristen once but had given up when she couldn't stop giggling before actually pulling the prank. She was surprised that she hadn't given herself up to Logan yet. But since he didn't even act like being locked in the stairway was a big deal, she kept telling herself that she could maintain her secret for a little while longer.

Over the next few minutes, she found it harder and harder to concentrate on her job. Even when she was on the phone with a client, all she could think about was Logan sitting a few feet away. He was slowly driving her mad.

It just wasn't fair. She could hear him clicking away on his computer like he didn't have a care in the world. She desperately wished she could call Kristen and tell her everything, but doubted she'd be able to sneak a few minutes alone to call her best friend until after work.

She glanced over to the corner and stared at the back of Logan's head for a moment. He'd changed a lot since the last time she'd seen him. Just before he'd moved away, he'd finally grown taller than her. At that point, her height had been something he had stopped making fun of her for. Sure, she could have poked fun at him for being a short kid for years, but she never seemed to have the right words. Nor had she wanted to stoop to his level.

Out of all the torture he'd subjected her to, none of it had hurt as badly as when he'd made fun of her parents getting a divorce. That's why it had thrown her off earlier that day when he'd acted like he cared when she'd told him about her parents' divorce. His kindness had thrown her for a loop.

After all, the divorce had been his favorite fuel for her ridicule besides her height. Maybe he really didn't know who she was?

"Ready to head out to our next appointment?" he said, breaking her thoughts. She was a little shocked to see him standing in front of her desk and realized she'd been staring at her computer screen blankly for a while.

She gathered up her things while trying to get Logan Miller out of her mind.

♦ ♦ ♦

Over the next few days, she couldn't seem to stop thinking about the man. Not only was he constantly sitting in her office, he seemed to cause the whole left side of her body to heat just knowing he was over in the corner.

Her office had never felt so cramped before. She kept trying to avoid being there, but her work almost always demanded it.

The list that Kristen and she had made burned in her mind. She'd found a few other opportunities to pay him back. Every time she would hesitate, but he would say or do something that justified her next act of revenge.

One day, he cornered her in the break room.

"I hear you've got a new listing in Genesee."

"Yes." She sipped the fresh cup of coffee she'd just poured. When he continued to move closer to her, she backed up until her butt hit the countertop. Frowning, she wondered why he still affected her that way.

"Mind if I tag along?" He reached behind her and took a mug from the cupboard, then poured himself a cup of coffee. His body continued to block her in the small corner of the break room.

"Sure." She wished he would take a step back. She was about to tell him that he'd better ride with her in her Jeep, since she knew the roads to the older property were terrible, but then he'd leaned a little closer to her, still trapping her against the countertop. She quickly glanced up and saw that his smile had grown. Her eyes traveled from his lips to his eyes and she could see a flash of mischief in them that she remembered all too well.

Instantly, a scene from her childhood played in her mind.

She'd gone out to her driveway and had plans to ride her new bike to meet Kristen at the park. But her bike was gone. She'd rushed in the house crying that it had been stolen. Her mother had insisted that maybe it would show up and that if it didn't, she would call the police the next day.

Since she hadn't wanted to disappoint Kristen, she'd walked all the way to the park. When she'd gotten there, she'd seen Logan riding her new bike through mud puddles with all his buddies laughing and egging him on.

When she'd marched over to him, he'd claimed he'd just "borrowed" her bike and he would have returned it. At that point, it was completely caked with mud and the back tire was flat.

Straightening her shoulders now, she returned from her memories and said, "You'll have to drive yourself. I need to run a personal errand after and won't be back to the office for a few hours."

He nodded and leaned his hip on the counter next to her.

She sidestepped around him and escaped into her office while chuckling. This was going to be a whole lot more fun than she'd first thought.

◆　◆　◆

Logan stared up at the hill and sighed. Why hadn't he thought to trade in his small sedan for an SUV? Better yet, he should get an old Jeep like Amy's.

The past evening's rain had caused the dirt road to become so muddy he guessed that even a four-wheel drive would have had issues.

Working in Cherry Creek, he'd never had the need for four-wheel drive. Every house he'd shown had been in a perfectly manicured neighborhood.

He supposed his little BMW could handle the trek up the hill, and since he was already running a few minutes late, he decided it would be worth a try.

His car made it halfway up the bumpy hill, then hit a patch of mud that was too deep for his smaller tires. Shaking his head in disgust, he felt his frustration grow as his back tires started spinning aimlessly.

Stepping out of his car, he groaned as his perfectly clean shoes sank in a deep puddle of mud. He supposed he deserved this, in the whole scheme of life. After all, he did use to be a hellion as a child. He understood now why she'd been so giddy when he'd agreed to drive himself.

Looking back up the hill, he decided to leave his car where it was and hike the rest of the way.

Maybe Amy would take mercy on him and help him get his car unstuck on the way out.

By the time he made it to the older house near the top of the hill, he'd removed his jacket and had sweat dripping down his back. He watched as Amy and an older man stepped out onto the front porch. He frowned when he saw that the man's hand was around her waist.

"Hey," he called out and they both looked toward him. Amy's smile fell away as he walked closer. The man dropped his arm from around her waist. The man looked familiar, but he couldn't place why or from where he would have known him. "Sorry I'm late. My car decided to stay behind." He chuckled. The long muddy walk had done him some good, cooling his frustration down.

"A drive like that requires four-wheel drive, son," the older man said with a shake of his head. "Bought this beauty last year." He walked over and tapped on the hood of a new SUV. "Nothing slows her down. Course"—he looked down at Logan's shoes—"city boy like you shouldn't be traipsing around in the mountains anyhow."

Logan laughed. "On that point, I think we both agree. Looks like I'll need to trade mine in and get something like this." He tilted his head and looked at the impressive piece of machinery that sat before them. "What kind of mileage does she get?"

The old man smiled and slapped him on the back and began talking to him about cars.

Logan chanced a glance at Amy and noticed that she hadn't moved from her spot on the porch. Her frown had increased and she'd even crossed her arms over those pretty breasts of hers. He could tell she wasn't too pleased that he'd made nice with the client. So, he decided to add a little more wood to the fire.

"Nice piece of property." He looked off toward the small cabin and the surrounding land. "I bet it's nice and peaceful up here during the winter."

"Yeah, I just don't care too much for the price tag attached to it." He scratched his full beard.

Logan's eyebrows shot up in question. "Where's the nearest neighbor?" He looked around, making a point of it.

"Not far enough, if you ask me."

"I bet it's about the only place on the hill that can say that." Then he thought of another tactic. "It's a shame how builders are flooding the area, popping up new neighborhoods left and right."

"Yeah, that's why I'm selling my place. Damn new construction of twelve houses just down the street from me."

"Amy, weren't you telling me that this place backed the Golden Gate Canyon State Park?" Logan turned toward her.

Amy glanced up at him from her paperwork and nodded slowly. "Yes, one of the largest sections of it, actually."

"Course, it takes a lot to get a permit to build on State Park land." He crossed his arms over his chest and felt a wave of satisfaction when he saw the man start to open to the idea. "Even then, they don't allow too many in."

"There is that." The man's eyes lit up. "I guess it wouldn't hurt to make an offer, now would it?" he asked Amy, and Logan watched as a smile flooded her face.

"No, Sam, it wouldn't. Why don't you come back inside and I'll write it up?"

The older man held out his hand. "Sam Lancaster."

"Sam, Logan Miller."

"Good to meet you, Logan. I own a couple car dealerships down in Denver." He reached into his pocket and handed Logan a business card. Logan did a double take as he glanced at it. He knew the dealership well. Then he realized why the man's face had looked so familiar to him. Everyone who lived in Denver knew who the man standing in front of him was.

"When you get ready to trade up, swing by and tell my boys I sent you. They'll give you the family discount." He winked at him and turned to walk into the house.

Amy opened the door for Sam, then for a brief moment, she glared at Logan. He just kept smiling at her and held the card like it was a medal.

CHAPTER
FOUR

It took Amy's Jeep only a few minutes to tug his car out of the muck. She waited as his BMW slid the rest of the way down the hill. When he was back on solid road, he waved to Amy and instantly headed toward Sam Lancaster's nearest dealership after making a call to his uncle and telling him he had to take the rest of the day off.

By nightfall, he was driving into his uncle's driveway in a new all-wheel-drive Audi Q7. This car was made for the mountains. Now, he was more than confident that he would never get stuck in the mud or the snow again.

The next morning when he drove up to work, Amy was just getting out of her Jeep and he parked in the spot next to hers.

"Well?" He stepped out and leaned on the side of his new ride. "What do you think?"

She chuckled. "Don't you think you went a little overboard?"

"You can never go overboard when it comes to power." He held up his key and locked his new machine.

He could tell she was trying not to laugh at him. She looked like she wanted to say something to him, but instead she just followed him toward the front doors.

He rushed to open the doors for her and enjoyed watching the way her hips swayed in the tight skirt she was wearing. When she entered her office, she removed her jacket, and for a moment, he couldn't blink or take his eyes off her. The white button-up blouse was sheer, leaving very little to the imagination. Her long hair was tied up in a loose bun with wisps falling around her face. Gold earrings dangled, catching the light from the open window, almost blinding him.

"You . . ." he cleared his throat, ". . . look very nice today."

Her smile was slow in coming. "Thanks, we have a big meeting in downtown Golden about one of the old Coors buildings."

He nodded, not really paying too much attention to what she was saying. His eyes just kept running over her body as she sat down behind her desk. Finally, her words sank through his haze of lust.

"Right, the McCormack Group."

She glanced up at him, her chin raised. She looked at him like he was slow and he cursed himself for not being able to pay attention.

"Yes, around eleven." It came out as a whisper, and he felt himself almost shiver at the sexy sound.

"I'll be there." Then he remembered his promise to his uncle that morning. "I'll meet you there; I have to help my uncle with a few things first."

"Do you have directions?" Her eyes were locked on his.

He frowned. "Isn't the meeting at the building in question?" He watched her nervously play with her watch and bracelets.

Her earrings danced in the sunlight as she shook her head slowly. "No, it's at McCormack Group's main office." She jotted down an address and handed him the paper.

He took it and shoved it into his pocket, not wanting to break eye contact with her.

"I'll see you there," he said. Just then her phone rang, pulling him out of the trance he'd been in.

As she answered it, he turned to go find his uncle.

◆ ◆ ◆

Amy watched Logan leave her office and tried to concentrate on the client talking to her on the phone. Her hands had been quivering throughout their entire conversation. She'd fiddled with her watch and bracelet just to keep them busy. Even her handwriting had been bad when she'd scribbled the wrong address down on her notepad. She sighed and answered her client's questions and was thankful she hadn't had to pay very much attention to the call.

When she hung up, she immediately called Kristen.

"I've done it." She rested her head on her desk and felt like laughing.

"What?" her friend asked, eagerly.

"Another two items from the list."

"Two? Tell me."

"Well, you know I've already done items four and seven," she whispered, glancing at the door nervously as she played with her bracelet.

"Yes." Kristen sounded excited. "So far so good."

She held back a giggle. "Well, I just pulled off item three and part two of six."

"Three and part two of six?" She could almost hear Kristen's mind working trying to remember what each one was.

"Three, for when, in junior high, he told me gym class was being held outside and I got locked out of the building for the entire period."

She heard Kirsten hold back a chuckle and frowned. "What?" Her eyes narrowed.

"Nothing." Her friend cleared her throat. "I was just imagining Logan getting detention like you had."

She smiled, imagining it herself. "Yeah, that would be nice."

34

"What's part two of six?" her friend interrupted as Amy imagined Logan sitting in detention in the spacious conference room down the hall.

"Well, I guess it was a little childish of me, but when he drove up in a new, shiny Audi this morning—you know after yesterday's number seven incident—I neglected to point out that he'd parked in a handicap spot. Knowing our building's security, his new car is already on the back of a tow truck."

"His car being towed is a whole lot bigger than your bike having a flat." She could tell that her friend was trying to hold back her laughter.

"It took my dad a whole year to fix that tire." She sat back, leaning her head against her chair. "I had to walk everywhere that entire summer."

"I remember. At least when I wasn't giving you a ride on my handlebars," Kristen added.

She smiled remembering. "Yeah, good times."

She could hear Kristen's sigh as she remembered it as well. Then she came back, her voice softer. "Maybe we shouldn't be doing this?"

Amy closed her eyes. "I've thought about that too. You know, I wasn't going to at first, but then he smiles at me with that same smile he would use right after he'd given my arm an Indian burn."

Kristen chuckled. "Okay, I'll leave it up to your good judgment."

"Besides, I haven't really done anything major like when he . . ." She shivered thinking about item number ten on their list.

"Don't even mention it," her friend broke in. "I still don't know what you're going to do to get him back for that one."

"Neither do I." She took a few deep breaths and tried not to let the guilty feelings start to overwhelm her. "Well, I'd better get going." She glanced at her watch. "Meetings all day."

"Okay, are we still on for dress shopping in a few weeks? I'm trying to set up the appointments at some bridal stores."

"Wouldn't miss it." She thought about shopping for her friend's wedding dress and a hint of sadness crept into her mind. She guessed it was due to the fact that she kept thinking she was losing the number one spot in Kristen's life, but then sanity would take over and she knew that no one could ever fill her spot as far as their friendship was concerned.

"Can you believe it? I'm getting married!"

"I know, I know." She felt her friend's excitement spread into her.

"Okay, I'll let you go. Ta-ta." She listened to Kristen hang up and couldn't help but smile all the way down to her car.

By the time she walked into the McCormack Group's offices, she was glancing over her shoulder repeatedly, waiting for Logan to spring out and expose her for what she'd done.

As the meeting went on, her nerves continued to grow. She was so wound up by the time everyone stood that her palms were so sweaty, she had to wipe them on her skirt before shaking anyone's hands.

As she walked out to her car, she was too preoccupied with guilt to notice the car parked next to hers.

"So"—the deep voice caused her to jump and spin around—"how'd the meeting go?" Logan was leaning on the hood of his car, looking quite comfortable. He'd removed his jacket and was wearing dark sunglasses, shielding his blue eyes from her view. It was so hard to tell his mood by just looking at his mouth and jaw.

"F-fine. Why didn't you come in?" She tried to act concerned, but since she hadn't thought to put on her sunglasses, she was sure he could read her guilt. She looked down at the keys and paperwork in her hands and shifted everything around so she wouldn't drop it.

"I actually just arrived." He stood up and walked toward her, taking the bulk of the paperwork from her hands.

"Oh?" She glanced up at him and took a deep breath, trying to hide her emotions. She twisted her watch a few times until she felt her nerves settle. His eyes followed the movement. "I guess I was a little too eager to show off my new car this morning and parked in a handicap spot." He looked over her right shoulder as he waved at someone behind her back.

"Oh, I hope your car wasn't towed," she said, glancing behind her as Nick, the head of the McCormack Group, started jogging toward them. The man was just a few years older than they, but already had a full head of silver hair. His athletic build and very tan skin told her that he cared a little too much about his physique.

"Logan." Nick held out his darker hand and Logan shook it with his own lighter one. "I thought that was you. What the heck have you been up to?"

"Getting my new car out of impound. Sorry I missed the meeting."

Nick looked between Logan and her a few times. "You're working for RMR now?"

"It's been a couple of weeks now." Logan reached up and removed his dark sunglasses and she saw his eyes for the first time. They were filled with laughter as he watched her face closely.

"Well that seals the deal then." Nick smiled and patted Logan on the shoulder. "I'm sure the board will feel much better knowing you'll be there to handle anything we need during this buy."

Instantly, Amy felt deflated and a little pissed. She threw her shoulders back as her chin rose a few inches, then as she started to open her mouth to retort, Logan beat her to it.

"Well, I'm just sitting on the sidelines for this one. Besides, Amy here is the best in the firm. I'm sure if there's anything that comes up, she's more than capable to handle it."

Nick glanced her way. "Yeah, sure. Hey, we were just about to hit lunch, want to . . ." He nodded toward some parked cars where the rest of the men from the meeting were standing around waiting.

Logan shook his head. "Can't. I've already got plans." He looked toward her and she felt like punching him. He made it seem like she had him on a leash—or worse, like they had plans together.

"Well," Nick said, glancing at her again, then back at Logan. "Another time. I'm sure glad you're back in town. We should shoot some hoops sometime."

"Look me up." He waved as Nick raced back to the rest of the group.

"Why did you do that?" she hissed as she reached for her car door.

"Do what?" He put his hand on her door, stopping her from opening it.

"Give him the impression that I had control over you."

"Trust me, that's not what he got from the conversation."

She frowned and tried to move his hand from her door. He leaned against it instead.

"So, where do you want to go for food?" he asked as he crossed his arms over his chest. "You're buying, since I just spent almost a week's salary getting Kelly out of impound."

Her eyes narrowed. "Kelly?"

His smile grew as he slipped on his sunglasses again. "Sure, why not. I remember how nice Kelly Steven's curves were in junior high."

She instantly felt her frustration grow.

"Oh come on. Don't you have a name for . . ." He patted her Jeep door and she frowned even more.

"Nothing I'm going to tell you." She took a step back, knowing she would explode with frustration if she stood too close to him.

He laughed. "Fair enough. Oh, come on. I'm starving after fighting with the towing company all morning. Besides, it's kind of your fault anyway."

She felt her stomach drop and held her breath as her head grew dizzy. A million questions raced through her mind. Did he know? Was he just playing with her? He had to know. After all, he remembered Kelly Steven. Why not her?

"I mean, I was distracted by those legs of yours." He made a point to tip down his sunglasses as his eyes raked over her legs. Then he whistled, and she couldn't stop herself from smiling.

"Fine, but we go Dutch." She yanked on her door, successfully dislodging him from his spot.

"I'll follow you." He hurried to his new car and she tried not to watch him too closely.

Did nothing get this guy down? She pulled out of the parking spot and watched as he followed her out of the lot.

CHAPTER
FIVE

The next day, she received a call from the McCormack Group with an official offer for the old Coors building. The offer was higher than she'd ever expected. Maybe now was the right time to ask Gary about becoming partner.

She tried not to dance a jig all the way to Gary's office to tell him the good news. She was also trying to build up the nerve to talk with him before she entered his office. In her excitement, she forgot to knock on his door and caught Gary and Leah in a heated embrace.

"Sorry." She backed out, giving the couple a moment to untangle themselves from each other.

"You can go in now, Amy," Leah said as she walked out of the door while adjusting her hair.

"Thanks. Sorry." She smiled at Leah.

"Oh, dear, no harm done." Leah winked at her.

"Hi." She walked up to Gary's desk and set the file down in front of him.

"What's this?" he asked, straightening his tie and looking down at the folder.

"An official offer on the old Coors building."

"What?" Gary's eyes jumped up to hers.

She nodded.

"Dare I look?" He rubbed his hands together and waited.

"Three point two." Her heart skipped again at the thought of the commission.

Gary whistled. "That's my girl." He stood up and wrapped her in his big arms and started spinning her around the room.

She was just about to ask Gary about taking her on as partner, when a voice from the doorway caused her to jump.

"I'm not interrupting anything, am I?" Logan stood just inside the door, a frown on his face as he took in the scene.

"There you are, my boy!" Gary pulled away from the hug and walked over to slap Logan on the back. "We were just celebrating Amy's big deal." Gary glanced over at her. She could see the pride and excitement in his eyes from across the room.

"Oh?" Logan said, still frowning in her direction.

Instantly she was on guard. What did he have to be upset about?

"Yup, my boy. This woman just landed the deal of the year." He slapped him again on the back and did a little skip as he walked back to his desk and picked up the folder she'd set down.

"What kind of deal?" Logan asked, walking more into the room.

"Oh, nothing short of a miracle. She took a run-down, almost-condemned building and sold it for three point two, cold." Gary danced around his chair while she laughed at him.

When she looked again, Logan's frown had been replaced by a smile that caused hers to fall away. His eyes were glued to her, instead of his uncle.

"This calls for a celebration!" Gary said loudly. "Drinks tonight." He rushed to the door. "Leah, tell the staff to meet at Main Street at five, if they can make it. I'm buying," he bellowed out the doorway.

In the all the years of working at RMR, Gary had bought drinks at Main Street Pub and Grill, a place a few doors down from their office, only six times. Four of which were all thanks to her.

"You're coming." He pointed at her, then turned to Logan and did the same.

Logan nodded, and she felt a lump in her throat. How was she going to possibly make it through a night of drinks with him there?

The next few hours seemed to tick by slowly. Logan sat in the small chair in the corner of her office, punching away at his computer and answering calls regarding potential real estate sales he'd hooked up earlier that week.

He was starting to build a list of his own clients and she couldn't wait for him to move into his own office space, even though she knew it wasn't going to be any time soon. RMR was housed on the second floor of the building and every possible space was already taken.

They would have to let someone go before he would have his own space. She frowned at the thought of that. Every person in the agency had earned his or her spot and she couldn't imagine going a day without each and every one of them.

"Something wrong?" Logan asked, leaning back in his chair.

She looked up at him. "No, just thinking." She twisted her bracelet as she thought about it further.

"It's about time to head out." He glanced at his watch. "I just need to file some paperwork." He walked over and waited as a stack of papers printed out. Then he tapped them straight and put them in a folder.

"Leah can file those for you," she said, mentally ticking off item number one on her list as she played with her watch. It was a small consolation prize knowing that the paperwork would most likely never be seen again. But after the sixth grade incident when he'd purposely tossed her backpack into the large, deep puddle, sufficiently ruining her science project that had been sealed inside, she was pretty sure he deserved it.

She watched him exit her office and smiled. Five down, five to go. She almost leaned back in her chair and propped up her feet as a reward, but stopped herself just in case he decided to come back or someone walked by her office and caught her.

◆ ◆ ◆

Logan followed the small crowd of people down the street to Main Street Pub and Grill, his eyes on Amy's back for most of the trip. She walked with a few of the other ladies from the office, and he watched her smile and laugh as they made their way down the narrow sidewalks. Her hair shone brightly in the dying sunlight, making him wish he knew how soft it would be in his hands.

When they finally made it to the pub, he glanced around and took stock. The glass doors opened up to a place that was small and cozy. They were greeted by music as a band played just inside the doors on a small stage area. Everyone from the office continued toward a seating area in the back that had been blocked off just for their party.

He made it a point to crowd closer to Amy so he would be seated next to her. When she noticed him sitting on her left, she frowned quickly and turned away, causing his smile to grow.

He was really enjoying how unsettled he could make her feel. Actually, he figured he'd take the little ruse as far as he could. After all, he was sure she had guessed that he knew who she was after he'd mentioned Kelly Steven, but so far she hadn't come out and said anything.

After the second round of drinks and hors d'oeuvres had been delivered, he caught Amy's eye and nodded toward the back, where a pool table sat in the middle of the room. "Care for a friendly game?"

Her eyes followed his to the far end of the room, then went back to his. "I don't think so," she said, taking another sip of her beer. He'd been surprised that she hadn't ordered a girlie drink like most of the other women from their office had.

"Scared I'll beat you?" He used the one tactic he knew would work on her.

"Not in the least." She set her almost empty beer down and played with her watch, twisting it vigorously.

"Then come on." He reached for her hand, pulled her up out of her seat, and started walking.

Her hand was small in his and he realized he could get used to holding it. He dropped it when they reached the table and he snatched up a cue stick. When he handed it to her, she took it and looked toward the front of the bar nervously.

"What shall we wager?" He took up a cue stick for himself, testing the length and weight of it slowly as he watched her make up her mind to play.

"How about money?"

"That's no fun." He thought about it. "Well, since we've got an outstanding bet for a date . . ." Her eyes heating, she quickly glanced at her coworkers around the table again, who were laughing and joking with one another. "How about dinner and drinks?"

"Gary's buying dinner and drinks tonight." Her eyes moved back to meet his.

"I wasn't talking about tonight." He leaned slightly on the table. She tilted her head as she twisted her watch. He was becoming accustomed to the motion.

"Come on." He could tell when she'd finally made up her mind.

"Fine, but I get to shoot first," she said.

He nodded. "Fair enough."

It was one of the hardest things he'd ever had to do in his life. Keeping his eyes from watching her tight little butt when she wiggled it as she got into position to hit the balls he'd lined up. She leaned over the table slowly and a strand of her perfectly coiffed hair fell into her eyes. The way he figured it, a few more drinks and she'd loosen the clip that held most of it away from her face. She'd already removed her blazer, giving everyone in the bar the beautiful view of her body.

His eyes moved over her arms as she lined up the cue for her shot. Instantly, he knew she'd get a few balls in.

Two solids shot into the end pockets, and when she moved around the table to line up the second shot, he guessed he was in trouble. Shot after shot, she sank her balls quickly. He leaned back and watched a pro at work. When, finally, after five turns, she missed a rather expert shot, he walked over to where she stood.

"I think I've been swindled." He leaned closer to her as she chuckled.

"You never asked if I could play," she said, a little breathless. He glanced down and noticed her breasts rise and fall with the excitement of the game.

"No, I suppose I didn't," he whispered. His hand reached out and brushed against her arm slightly. "A mistake I won't be making again."

Her smile faltered as she took a step back. "Your turn."

He moved to lean in, but straightened when his uncle approached.

"There you two are." He could tell that his uncle was on his way to being drunk. His round cheeks had a hint of red in them and his arm was slung over Leah's shoulders. "We were just looking for you guys."

"Just playing a friendly game of pool," he said, before striking his first ball.

"Oh! That's not such a good idea with this one." Gary pointed with his hand, which was holding an almost empty beer mug. The golden liquid nearly sloshed over the edge. "She's a real shark." He chuckled. "Took me for a few hundred dollars last time."

"Yeah, you were the one that insisted on playing for money," Amy added.

He laughed. "So true. Learned my lesson, though. Haven't played her since."

"We're not playing for money," he said, sinking another ball quickly.

"Oh?"

"Gary, I think everyone wants another round," Leah said, using all her strength to hold the larger man up.

"Oh! Right you are. I'll make sure to send the waitress back to get your drink order." His uncle and Leah meandered back toward the front, which had grown much louder than before.

"They make a cute couple," Amy said, sighing as she leaned against the table.

His eyebrows shot up and he glanced at their backs. "Who? Them?" He turned to her and saw her nod.

"Why do you think he's kept her around all these years?" She giggled and downed the rest of her beer.

His eyes traveled back to the table with his coworkers. He frowned. He'd never imagined that his uncle had been involved with anyone.

"Are you going to hit that ball or sulk about your uncle's love life?" She leaned on the table as the waitress delivered two more beers.

He lined up for the shot and smiled as he sank two balls. When he moved around the table to line up for the next shot, Amy was there, her hip resting on the edge of the table as she sipped her beer. Her leg was swaying to the music as her eyes watched him move.

Instantly, he felt heat spread throughout his body from the looks she was giving him. He stopped in front of her, then reached over, lifted his beer mug, and took a drink, letting the cold liquid cool him down.

When his eyes met hers again, he saw her cheeks flush and her eyes heat, matching his own. He leaned closer. Her leg stopped moving and she set her beer down. He was a breath away from her—so close, he could smell the soft scent of her perfume mixed with the aroma of beer. For some reason, the combination was intoxicating.

His eyes moved to her lips as her tongue darted out and licked her full bottom lip. He held back a groan, watching the sexy movement.

"Logan?" she said in a soft whisper. "Shoot."

He blinked a few times, images of what he wanted to do to her flashing through his mind.

"Shoot the ball." She pushed him and got him moving.

He'd been clenching the cue stick tightly in his hands, so he relaxed his fingers and slowly made his way around the table to take the next shot, an easy one. Since he was still distracted at the thought of her lips, he missed.

He thought he heard her chuckle as she edged her way around the table and took the next shot. He stood back and, this time, didn't avoid looking where he wanted as he sipped his beer.

CHAPTER
SIX

When Amy sank the eight ball, she felt a wave of excitement rush through her, as it always did. She loved to win.

Looking over and seeing the slight frown on Logan's face was icing on the cake.

"Looks like I win." She walked over, picked up her waiting beer, and took a sip of the warm liquid.

Then he moved so quickly, she almost yelped. His hand was on her hip as he pulled her close. Her hand went to his chest, squished between them.

He smiled down at her. "Looks like I owe you drinks . . . some other time." He whispered the last part.

Her heart jumped in her chest and she thought she felt his matching beat against her hand. Her eyes went to his lips and she found it hard to look away.

"What . . ." She didn't get any further as a crowd of loud people approached the pool table. Logan dropped his arms and quickly moved away, walking over to pick up his beer.

"See, they're done playing," someone said loudly.

She stepped aside, making sure to take her beer with her as the crowd of people took over.

"The place gets a little crowded on game night." She glanced toward the large-screen television that tonight's game was playing on.

He took her elbow and steered her across the front room to where the rest of their group had gone to cheer on the game. They had ordered more food and when she sat down, she reached for some chips.

"Want something more?" Logan said, leaning in to her ear.

She glanced at him and he pointed toward a menu.

"No, I'm not really hungry." She lied. The funny thing was, she was starved. Just not for anything on the menu.

She really needed to get out more often. It had been almost five months since she'd gone out on a date. Even then, it had been a double date with Kristen and Aiden and a friend of his, who, by the end of dinner, she had had zero interest in pursuing.

Maybe Kristen was right. Was she being too picky? She glanced around the table at RMR's employees. There were two men she'd dated in the past here tonight. She held in a groan of embarrassment as she watched both men now. John had been the first to ask her out when she'd started working for Gary.

John was a year older than she and a few inches shorter, but she didn't allow that to matter, much. It was where he'd taken her on their first date that had turned her off. He'd actually thought she would enjoy going to a strip club.

She held back a chuckle as she watched him try to flirt with their waitress. Shaking her head, she sipped on her beer and glanced at Ron, the second man from RMR who had asked her out. Ron had been nice enough, and in all honesty, she couldn't really remember why she hadn't clicked with him.

He was a lot shyer than John, and Logan for that matter. Tilting her head, she thought about it. Ron was actually shyer than anyone she'd ever met before. He was good-looking enough, with his rich chestnut hair, green eyes, and those dimples on either side of his mouth. Who could deny a man with those dimples?

Currently Ron was sitting along the back wall alone, eating a Reuben sandwich. Just a glance at the sandwich caused her stomach to growl loudly. She doubted if Ron had ever spoken to anyone at their table for any amount of time and wondered why he even came along to these events. Maybe it was the free food? She watched him pick up his sandwich and take a large bite.

"I'm sure the rest of us can leave you two alone?" Logan whispered in her ear.

"Hmm?" She turned toward him.

He nodded to where Ron sat by himself, eating the rest of his sandwich. She looked back at Logan and laughed.

"I guess I'm a little hungry." She waved to the waitress, who looked relieved to leave John's advances to make her way over to Amy.

She ordered the Reuben sandwich and wasn't surprised when Logan requested the same thing.

"So, is there something between you two?" He glanced again at Ron.

"Ron's okay, but we just never really hit it off."

Logan was silent for a while, so she glanced his way and saw him frowning in Ron's direction. Turning her body, she leaned her elbow on the table and smiled at Logan. She could swear he was looking at the other man with jealousy.

"What about you?" She waited until his eyes returned to her. "I'm sure there're a lot of broken hearts in your past." She tilted her head and waited for his answer.

"A few, but nothing serious." She could see the lie in his eyes and remembered the conversation they'd had while driving to the house showing with the Lufts. Her eyebrows lifted in doubt as she stared at him. "Well, maybe one or two," he admitted.

She waited and when he didn't continue, she asked, "Why is it that men never think it's serious?"

It was his turn to look at her with doubt. "Who says we don't?"

"You just did."

"Well, in most cases, that's true. These two"—he took another sip of his beer—"I was the one broken in the end."

"Oh?" She watched him and waited.

"You really want to hear about them?" he asked.

"Why not?" She was hoping he'd slip up and admit he knew who she was. Or maybe she just wanted to hear more about him.

He leaned back and crossed his arms over his chest. "Fine, but you asked for it," he said as the waitress set their sandwiches in front of them.

When he started to eat in silence, she nudged his leg with hers. "Go on."

He glanced at her. "I was hoping to eat this in peace."

She ate a few bites, then nudged his leg again until he started talking.

"Fine, Bella was in some of the same classes in CSU. We hit it off and a few months later, got engaged."

She almost choked on the sip of beer she was swallowing. He dropped his sandwich and patted her back a few times.

"Sorry." She took another sip of beer. "Go on." She picked up her sandwich and took another bite.

"About three weeks into our engagement, I walked into the apartment to find her in bed with one of our professors."

She swallowed the bite of sandwich wrong, and he ended up having to smack her on the back once again.

"Maybe I should wait until we're done eating before I tell you about Tiffany."

She shook her head and felt her eyes water. "I'm okay," she managed to say, but pushed her almost empty plate aside. "Go on." She moved her beer aside as well, then took a large sip of cool water instead.

He shoved the last bite of his sandwich into his mouth then took a drink of his beer.

"I met Tiffany when I worked at CCR. She was the boss's daughter and naturally had her pick of men at the agency." He sighed, and she could tell he was struggling with getting the story out.

"What happened?" she asked. She could see the hurt in his eyes and felt a little guilty for pushing him to talk. But she wanted to know more.

He glanced at her, the frown still on his lips. "We started seeing one another and then we didn't."

"Something must have happened?"

"Apparently I wasn't edgy enough to piss off her old man, so she started seeing the women in the agency instead."

She felt her mouth drop open, then she couldn't stop the laughter that followed.

"Oh, that's great. I tell you about my heartbreak, and you laugh." He crossed his arms over his chest defensively.

She bit her lip as a few faces around the table turned to look at them. Then she was wiping her eyes with her napkin as the laughter took over.

Logan, for his part, continued to stare at her like she'd lost it.

"You . . ." She swallowed the laughter. "You're the one with a broken heart, not them?"

"That's what you asked, right?" His voice was low.

"Not necessarily. Were you madly in love with them?" She leaned on the table and watched him closely.

He looked at her, then slowly shook his head. "I have never been in love."

She made a whooshing noise and tapped him on the shoulder. "I doubt that."

Just then she realized she'd had too much to drink. She never made noises like that, not unless she was toasted. Sitting up, she couldn't tear her eyes away from Logan's smile. Taking stock of herself, she realized her hair was falling in front of her eyes, and she reached up to push it away.

"No." He stopped her, his hand encasing her own smaller one. "I like seeing it down." He leaned closer and tugged until the clip that held her hair up came loose. Her long hair flowed around her face and shoulders. "There, much better." Her eyes locked onto his lips and she wished, for just a moment, that she was the kind of girl that could let herself enjoy the moment.

◆　◆　◆

After spilling his heart to Amy in their private conversation, it seemed the entire group disbanded. First the skinny guy who'd sat alone in the corner left, then Logan's uncle and Leah. Then more. He continued to talk with Amy as the tables around them emptied.

Finally, she looked around and noticed that they were the last of their group still there.

"I'd better . . ." She glanced down at her watch. "Oh, how did it get to be so late?"

"Time flies." He stood up and helped her pull her blazer on. He was sad to see those sexy shoulders of hers get covered up with the heavy material.

"Thanks," she murmured.

"Here, I'll walk you back to the office parking lot." He held out his arm for her. She hesitated for just a moment, then took his arm.

When he opened the pub door for her, she glided through and he followed her out into the balmy night. There was a cool breeze that sent her hair blowing into her eyes. She tucked the loose strands behind her ears.

"I didn't mean to laugh at your heartache," she said as they made their way back up the hill.

"I know. I guess I've never really thought of my story as funny before. But, it's been two years now, so I'm totally over it."

"I had a boyfriend cheat on me in high school once."

He glanced at her. "Did you cut out his heart?"

She chuckled. "No, he works at the local tire shop and has been in and out of jail for drunk driving. I guess you can say it was for the best."

"Yeah, Tiffany finally settled down last year and is currently engaged to a man her father approves of."

"And Bella?" she asked.

"Married the professor and has two kids."

"I guess when it's right . . ." She broke off.

"You ever come close?" They stopped walking when they reached the empty parking lot. Only her Jeep and his new SUV were parked in the dimly lit lot.

Then he leaned against the side of her Jeep, relaxed and waiting for her answer, proving to her that he wasn't ready for the night to end just yet.

She sighed and shook her head. "No close calls for me."

"Oh?" He smiled. "For some reason I can't imagine someone hasn't tried to tie you down yet."

"They would have to get close to me first." Then her smile fell away. "I mean . . ."

He reached out to take her hips in his hands, then he pulled her closer. He felt her breath hitch as her hands rose to his chest. "Like this?" he asked softly.

She nodded just before he dipped his head and brushed his lips across hers. He'd been fantasizing about kissing those lips for weeks. Ever since he'd seen her nibble on them nervously as she made her presentation that first day.

He felt her body melt against his and deepened the kiss until he felt his own catch fire. Then, he stepped back and dropped his arms.

"Are you okay to drive?" He watched her eyes focus as she nodded. "Good night." He turned toward his car before he did anything stupid like follow her home.

"Logan?" she called out to him. He stopped and looked over his shoulder at her. "Good night." She climbed into her Jeep and drove away slowly.

CHAPTER
SEVEN

By the end of the month, she was a little disappointed that the Lufts hadn't made an offer on the house in Clear Creek yet. She had even called and left them a couple of messages, just in case. She couldn't deny any longer that there was a big possibility she'd been wrong about the young couple. Which only upset her even more, since she had to look at the back of Logan occupying her space every day.

She was finding it more and more difficult to work with Logan sitting in her office, especially after that kiss. Not to mention, she suspected he was listening in on her phone conversations and purposely going out of his way to accompany her on every showing she had.

Not only was he a big distraction, but she couldn't stop her mind from replaying every moment of torture he'd caused her in her youth, and now he was pouring on the charm like he was actually interested in her. The strange part was that her body was starting to respond to him. Which only made her even madder that her mind could be betrayed so easily. Maybe it was the kiss that had damned her? She could feel his warm lips on hers if she thought about that night. And she found herself thinking about it all too often.

When that Friday evening finally rolled around, she was relieved that she would be free of him for a couple of days. At least until he glanced over his shoulder and smiled at her.

"Looks like I win the bet." He leaned back in his chair, looking very comfortable in the small space. He'd removed his jacket and had rolled up the sleeves of his white shirt.

"We still have an hour to go." She glanced down at her watch and noticed that it was closer to forty-five minutes left in the wager. "Are you going to tell me what led you to believe the Lufts wouldn't make an offer?"

He laced his fingers behind his head. The motion caused his shirt to stretch tight over his chest and she found her eyes roaming over every inch of him. "They're expecting."

Her eyes flew to his and she nodded slowly. "Yes, I know. What does that have to do with them buying this house?"

"Can you imagine raising a child, who in eight months to a year will likely be crawling and walking, in a house built on a cliff?"

She blinked a few times and felt her spirits fall. She'd never thought of it that way. She started playing with her bracelets. The jingle sounds filled the office.

"I see by your look that you hadn't." His smile grew.

She felt the anger from deep within her. "Why didn't you mention this earlier? I could have shown them another house."

"Because then I wouldn't have a date with you tomorrow night."

She glared at him. "And you still don't." She turned her chair around and started to pick up the phone to call the Lufts. There were so many other homes she could offer to show them that were better suited for a young family.

Before she could dial the first number, her chair was spun around.

"Hold on." He leaned closer, his hands resting on the chair's arm-rests. "A deal is a deal," he said close to her face.

"You could have lost this agency a lot of money, all because you wanted to gamble on a date?" Her eyes narrowed. "You need to know when to put childish games aside, Mr. Miller." She tried to turn her chair back around, but he held her still. The phone receiver was still clenched in her hand and she felt like tossing it at him. "Let go," she said under her breath.

"You haven't lost the deal yet. I emailed them a few other, more appropriate listings just yesterday." He smiled as his eyes roamed over her face.

"You did what?" She felt her body begin to vibrate with even more anger. "These are my clients." She pushed herself up from her chair, causing him to take a step back as she let the phone dangle from the side of her desk. Then she shoved a finger into his chest. "You had no right. Who do you think you are?"

He backed up a step. Then held his hands up and tried to open his mouth.

"No!" She glared at him, not wanting to hear his voice at the moment. "I don't know how they handled these kind of situations at CCR, but this is not how we do business at RMR. It is never okay to take clients away from another agent." She turned, picked up her phone, and slammed it down. Reaching over, she closed her laptop and picked up her purse. She couldn't stand to be in the same room with him anymore.

Marching out of the room, without another word or look aimed in his direction, she left him standing behind her desk with his mouth hanging open. She was too revved up to stop and talk with Gary as she passed him in the hallway on her way out of the building.

As she drove out of the parking lot, a lot of her anger turned to hurt, just as it had always done when he'd pulled a prank on her or teased her.

She didn't know why she allowed him to have this effect on her, especially since she hadn't let anyone else affect her like that since then.

She knew he'd been playing her. Why had she fallen for that kiss? She should have seen his betrayal coming, but she hadn't.

Her mind raced over the last few items on the list that Kristen and she had made, wishing there was something she could do to pay him back for this new infraction. But no matter how much she thought about it, she just couldn't come up with anything.

She parked her Jeep outside of Kristen's office and glanced down at her watch. Her friend should be coming out of the building soon, so she texted her.

I'm outside. Wanna get some drinks?

It took a few minutes for Kristen to reply.

On my way out now. Yes, Aiden is stuck in a meeting, so . . . good timing.

When Kristen rushed across the street, her long curly hair flowing wildly behind her like her multicolored skirt, Amy couldn't stop from smiling at her friend. She looked happy and in love.

"Hey," Kristen said, making sure her skirt was inside the Jeep before shutting the door. "Where to?" She glanced over at Amy, then frowned. "What's up?" She turned her entire body toward her friend.

"What else?" Amy groaned and leaned her head back against the headrest.

"Logan?" Kristen said just as Amy nodded. "What did he do this time?"

Amy rolled her eyes. "Drinks first, then I'll tell you."

Kristen reached over and squeezed her hand. "We'll make it through this."

"Right, just like last time."

"Maybe he'll move again," Kristen suggested.

"One can only hope," she prayed out loud.

◆　◆　◆

Logan watched Amy storm out of the office. He knew better than to stop a woman on a rampage. After all, that's how a few of his relationships had ended over the years.

When she was gone, he sat back down at his computer and finished his work. When his uncle walked into the room a few minutes later, worry written on his face, he knew he wouldn't get any more work done for the day.

"What have you done now to upset Amy?" His uncle leaned on the side of her desk and put his hands in his trouser pockets.

Logan laughed. "Hell if I know."

His uncle just looked at him. So he threw his hands up, providing a better answer.

"Fine, I might have maneuvered her into going out with me."

"You're so desperate, you have to play games to get girls to go out with you now?"

"When you know what kind of history we have . . . yeah. This was the only way to convince her," he admitted.

"Seems to me coming right out and saying you're sorry would be easier."

"Easier, but not as fun." He couldn't admit to his uncle that it was really fear preventing him from apologizing to her for years of torment. Fear of messing things up with Amy again.

"Boy," his uncle walked over and patted him on the shoulder. "You don't know what you're in for. Amy has done a lot of growing herself. She's not the little girl whose pigtails you used to tug on anymore."

"Trust me, I know that." He thought about the differences in her and how much he'd been turned on by them.

"She's cautious," his uncle said.

"I've noticed." He couldn't remember her ever acting that way when they were younger, but then again, he hadn't paid attention to her then as he was now.

"She won't take being treated badly lying down."

Logan leaned back in the chair.

"She's . . ." His uncle shook his head. "I won't stand here warning you anymore. I can tell you're not going to listen to a word I say." He laughed. "What do you say you take an old man out for dinner so I won't have to eat alone?"

Logan shut down his computer and stood. "Fine, but you're buying."

His uncle slapped him on the shoulder. "Fine, but you're buying the beer."

They headed out and Logan drove to one of his uncle's favorite Mexican restaurants. When the smell of the food hit him, he realized he'd been starving. As the soft music floated around him and the warm atmosphere surrounded him, along with the refreshing taste of a good imported beer, he thought about how he had always had a good time with his uncle. Even though the man had been missing for most of his childhood, he still felt close to him.

Maybe because he reminded him so much of himself. Gary Bartolo was a joker. Most people in his office didn't know it, but the man knew how to make people laugh.

By the time their dinner was served, his uncle had their waitress crying with laughter.

"Kill 'em with laughter, son," he said, smiling over the table at him. "No matter what's going on in life, there isn't a situation that can't be solved or gotten over with a good laugh."

He thought about it and didn't want to contradict him. Not since they were both working on their second beer.

Logan had used humor most of his life to mask the pain of his childhood. He knew he'd been a little devil growing up. He could easily blame it on the fact that his parents had never really been around. He'd gotten away with anything.

Looking back at it, he no longer could justify the terrible things he'd done as a child. One of the main reasons he'd taken the job with his uncle was because Amy worked there. A small part of him wanted to set things right with her. Now, however, he couldn't deny the attraction he felt every time he watched her straighten her skirt or tuck a strand of her long hair behind her sexy little ears.

He knew the underlying reason he let her get away with the pranks she was pulling on him now. Guilt. Pure and simple. He kept telling himself that if she played out her revenge, it would be easier for them to be on the same level. But part of him had to admit that he just couldn't seem to break his habit of riling her. Something in him loved to see her face flush and her eyes heat. Not that he would do anything as bad as tossing firecrackers at her again, but just knowing that he could do or say the smallest thing and see her react had him going out of his way to poke at her.

He had every intention of getting what he wanted, and what he wanted was Amelia Walker.

CHAPTER
EIGHT

Amy stormed in her front door and felt a little better after slamming it behind her. Knowing no one was around to hear or see her tantrum didn't stop her from feeling satisfied either.

Because of Logan, she'd spent her entire day off at the office, working. Now, not only was she annoyed, but she was tired and hungry as well.

Since the office only had a small vending machine filled with every sugary snack known to man, she had skipped lunch. Of course it had been hard to resist a quick treat, and at one point, she had stood in front of the machine and cursed herself for gaining five pounds last winter.

She always gained weight during the colder months of Colorado's winters. She supposed it was her body's way of trying to go into hibernation by telling her to eat all those holiday treats everyone always brought into the office. She struggled to lose the weight every spring no matter how many times she promised herself she'd cut out the sweets.

It had taken all her willpower to walk away from the snack machine and nibble on the granola bar she'd stocked in her desk drawer instead.

But now, as she was mentally running through other food options, her doorbell rang.

Thinking it was Kristen, she called out, "Come in," as she walked back into her kitchen to scrounge up a meal.

Her head was buried deep in her fridge when she heard a man clear his throat behind her. She jumped and her hand knocked against the top shelf, dislodging a large bottle of wine she'd half drunk the night before. The bottle twirled a few times before finally tipping over and falling off the shelf onto her foot.

She found herself hopping up and down on one foot and holding her hurt hand to her chest. She glared at Logan, who was standing less than a foot behind her. "What are you doing here?" she demanded.

"Are you okay?" He looked down at her foot as she continued to hop on the other one. "Here." He walked over and took her arm and led her to a kitchen stool. "Sit." He pushed her shoulders lightly until she fell back. Then he shocked her by pulling her bare foot up and rubbing his hand over the red mark.

"Ouch!" She tried to tug her foot away.

"It doesn't appear to be broken," he said, still looking down at her bruised foot.

"Of course it's not broken." She pushed on him, until he moved back. "Are you going to answer me?"

He leaned back and smiled at her. "I'm here to collect."

"Collect what?" She frowned down at him.

"Your debt." He finally released her foot and she felt a chill run up her leg from losing the warmth of his hands.

"Debt?" She blinked a few times.

"Dinner."

She felt all the anger from the day before rush into her again. "You've got to be . . ."

"Unless you want to go back on a bet?" He stood up and leaned a little closer to her. She could smell his aftershave and for a moment she lost her train of thought.

Shaking her head, she swallowed hard and tried not to let how sexy he looked in a pair of worn jeans and a button-up shirt affect her.

"Good." He held out his hand for her to take. She looked at it. His eyebrows rose as he waited for her to move.

"How did you find out where I live?" she asked, putting her hands together.

"I'm not stalking you. It's a small town still. Besides, my uncle told me."

She thought about it, then took his hand and let him help her stand up off the stool.

"How does your foot feel?" He looked down at it.

"Fine." She wiggled her toes and was happy that most of the pain was gone. He walked over and picked up the bottle of red wine that had rolled toward her dishwasher.

"Nice." He smiled down at the label. "How about we grab a bottle of this at Bono's?"

Her stomach growled loudly at the thought of a large cheese pizza at her favorite Italian restaurant.

"My thoughts exactly." He nodded to her feet. "You'll want some shoes on first." Since it had been her day off, she'd worn cotton capris and a light cream shirt. She walked over to slip on a pair of practical, but stylish shoes.

She didn't own a pair of old jeans like the ones he was wearing. They looked as comfortable as her pants did, but his fit him a lot better. Not to mention that when he faced away from her, her eyes zeroed in on his butt and she had a difficult time looking away.

Damn, it was going to be hard having dinner with him while she was still trying to hate him so much.

♦ ♦ ♦

Logan couldn't concentrate on the short drive to Bono's. He didn't know how she still looked so fresh when she'd spent the entire day at the office working. Even when she'd been hopping up and down on one foot in her kitchen, she'd looked perfect. Her hair had fallen across her face in the frenzy, but she had still looked beautiful, flushed and breathless.

Something tugged at him to see if he could make her come undone a little. To see what she would look like with her hair messed up from his fingers, or better yet, fanned out on his pillow after a night of making love.

He shook his head and growled when he almost drove past the turn to the popular restaurant. He'd missed Bono's while living in Cherry Creek. The small strip mall was in an older part of town, and Bono's had been a staple there for as long as he could remember.

The pizza was some of the best he'd ever had. Although it was the good times he'd spent hanging out with his junior high buddies near the back of the dark restaurant that he remembered the most.

He threw his new Audi into park and before Amy could get out, rushed around to open her door for her.

As he helped her out of the car, he added, "I haven't been here in years." He opened the front door of the restaurant and the smells hit him, flooding his mind with even more good memories.

"How long have you been back in Golden?" she asked as they sat at a table near the back.

"Just the month." He looked down at the menu.

"You haven't been back since you left?" she asked, pushing her menu aside and leaning on the table, watching him.

"Nope. I kept meaning to come, but . . ." he sighed, ". . . life just got in the way."

She sat back when the waitress walked over and poured them each a glass of water. "Hey, Amy," the teenager said.

"Hi, Rachelle." She smiled up at the redhead.

"Do you guys know what you want?" she asked him.

"We'll start with a bottle of red wine." Logan watched Rachelle walk away to the bar to get their wine. "Not much in town has changed since I've been away."

"Did you expect it to?"

He tilted his head and thought about it as his eyes ran over her slowly. When her face heated, he said in a low voice, "I had kind of hoped they'd fill in the pothole on Main."

She took a drink of her water and he could see her color return to normal. "It's been filled at least a dozen times in the same number of years. Each time we have a big snowfall, it sinks in again."

"Go figure."

"There's the new statue along the Riverwalk."

"I haven't seen it yet." He loved the Riverwalk in downtown Golden. It had been one of the best places he had escaped to as a child.

"I noticed it the last time I went canoeing."

He couldn't hide his interest. "You canoe?"

He wondered what other secrets she was hiding. It was hard to imagine her rushing down a Colorado river in a small boat. The wind and water spraying her face.

He leaned forward. "Maybe it's about time I got back in the water myself."

When the waitress walked up again, he looked over at Amy. "Large cheese okay with you?"

"As long as we start off with some cheesy bread. I'm starved."

"Sounds good to me."

Over the next few minutes, he asked her question after question about herself. Why she chose her career path. What schools she went to. More about the men she'd dated.

When he tried to get a little more out of her about her family, she closed up and started asking him questions.

All of which he answered willingly. She was playing the part of not knowing him well, so he figured he'd keep playing along with her game.

He didn't want to rock the boat too much, and chance spooking her so soon. He was amused when she started asking questions about his family and acting like she didn't know that he had a younger sister or that his father had been away in the military for most of his childhood.

Just as he had always done as a child, he omitted the family secret: that his father would come home and beat him.

♦ ♦ ♦

By the time their pizza was delivered, Amy was completely relaxed, enjoying their conversation. It was hard to imagine there was another side to Logan that she hadn't seen before. She knew that she'd done a lot of growing up in the almost thirteen years since she'd seen him last, but she had never really thought about him changing as well. In her mind, Logan was still the bully with torn jeans from her childhood.

She could see how much he'd changed as she sat across from him in the small restaurant. His shoulders were broader than they had been in school. His face still looked the same, but he'd lost a lot of his childhood chubbiness. His chin was stronger looking, and the slight stubble he had on his face added a hint of danger. His arms were full of muscles that hadn't been there before either. Not to mention that butt of his. She didn't remember her mouth drooling at it before.

She watched him eat the pizza like it was the best thing on earth, and it was. She savored her slice just as much.

It surprised her to see that there was only one piece left by the time their bottle of wine was gone. She'd lost track of time while he joked about a few jobs he'd had in high school.

"So, that's why I chose to be a Realtor."

"Because you couldn't flip burgers?" she joked.

"And, because I decided I couldn't stand to know what happened to my food before it reached my table."

She cringed. "Don't remind me. I spent a summer waiting tables at the Mexican place down the street."

"Something else we have in common."

Her smile fell away and she frowned down at her empty wine glass. What was she doing? She'd let her guard down for a moment. This was Logan Miller. Her lifelong nemesis. The boy who had caused her more pain than all her ex-boyfriends combined.

For the remaining time in the restaurant, she sat back and listened to his stories, trying to figure out what his game was.

She thought of a few ways to test him, to see if he was pulling something but didn't know if she had enough nerve to try any of them. That was until he brought up the Lufts. Then she had no problem testing the waters.

She listened to him explain how he'd sent the email out with her contact information, but it didn't negate the fact that he'd gone behind her back.

Her opportunity arrived as they were walking out the door. Heather Kurtz happened to be walking into Bono's on the arm of a man twice her age. Since graduating from college, Heather had been gold digging. Trying to find anyone who could keep her in her Versace and Valentino. So far, she'd gone through every man in town near her own age and had begun to move on to men twice her age. She was slowly making her way through the seniors and was currently wooing Mr. Wilkens, a local jewelry store owner, who for his part, seemed to be enjoying the extra attention he got by dating a younger woman.

"Heather." Amy stopped just outside the doors. Normally, she wouldn't have paused to hold the door open for the woman, but with Logan in tow, she couldn't pass up the opportunity to see how he would react. She knew she would be outing herself, but at this point, the game was starting to get old. Heather glanced at her. No hint of recognition crossed the blonde's eyes. "It's me, Amy Wa—er, Amelia Craig."

"Oh, yes." She could still see the girl didn't know who she was. Even after they had spent years together in the same school and even at one point played volleyball together. "How nice to see you again."

"You remember Logan Miller?" Heather's eyes traveled to Logan, who had just stepped out the door. Instantly, Amy regretted her actions when she saw Heather's eyes heat and recognition spark.

"Logan!" The woman squealed before tossing herself into his arms. "When did you get back?"

Logan's eyes moved over to Amy's and Amy thought she saw fear behind the blueness.

"Last month. I'm working for my uncle over at . . ."

"Oh, that's simply wonderful." She glanced at Mr. Wilkens quickly. Then she leaned forward and whispered loud enough for Amy to hear. "We'll definitely have to get together sometime. Call me." She purred the last words as she looked directly at Amy. Then she turned and wrapped an arm through the older man's and walked into the building.

"You did that on purpose," Logan growled at her after the door shut.

"I don't know what you mean." She bit her bottom lip to hide the slight smile from him. It had felt good to see him squirm as he'd caused her to do over the last few weeks.

His eyes narrowed as he took her hand in his. Instead of heading back to his car, Logan started down the street.

CHAPTER NINE

With Amy's hand in his own, Logan walked toward the river that ran directly through town. So much had actually changed in Golden that he hadn't noticed before. They had resurfaced the streets and had new road signs hanging on every streetlight. Some of the old buildings had been remodeled and housed new shops, while others had simply been torn down.

He kept her hand in his as they walked down the stairs to the edge of the water. It was now early August, and even with the sun gone over the mountains for the night, the temperatures were still warm enough that there was a bead of sweat rolling down his back.

They were in luck when he spotted an empty bench positioned along the edge of the rushing water. When they sat down, he gently placed his arm over her shoulders.

"There, this is nice." He glanced her way. When he turned toward her, she avoided him by turning her head in the opposite direction. "Do you want to tell me why you tried to get me smothered by Heather Hurtz?"

He watched her fight the smile as he used Heather's school nickname.

"You know why?" She turned and faced him. "I don't like playing games."

He nodded. "I remember that about you," he added as he pulled her closer.

"So, you do remember?" She pushed him away as she crossed her arms over her chest and glared at him, a frown forming on her lips.

"I remember lots of things." He brushed his hand through her hair as she tried to swat him away. "I remember the summer you wore those silk shorts that used to be in style. They always drove every boy in the neighborhood crazy. Including me."

Her frown grew, but for a moment, he thought he heard her breath hitch.

"I remember the first day you showed up at school wearing a bra." He smiled as he remembered how she'd fiddled with the straps most of the day. "I never knew simple white cotton could be so sexy." His hand cupped the back of her head and drew her closer.

"I remember doing this for the first time . . ." He leaned closer and placed his lips on hers softly.

When he pulled back after the kiss, he grabbed hold of her hands. "I also remember what came afterward. You're not going to slug me again, are you?"

"You deserved it, since you were dared."

"What?" He kept hold of her hands, just in case.

"Taylor Franklin dared you to kiss me on the bus." She almost growled it out.

"No, no one dared me." He watched her struggle with the new knowledge.

"Why did you then?" she whispered.

"Because you were sitting in the back seat, all by yourself, pouting." His smile grew when her lips turned down in the cute pout he remembered so well. "Yeah, just like that." He brushed his thumb over her soft bottom lip and started to lean closer to her. "Drove me crazy back then." He ran his lips over the sweet curve once more.

"I . . . I don't understand." She shook her head slightly.

"You never did." He felt like there was too much ground for him to cover with her. Besides, he wasn't sure he was ready to admit anything more that evening. He wasn't ready and he was pretty sure she wasn't either.

Leaning back, he knew that any further discussion on why he'd acted the way he had would cause problems, and he didn't want to start a fight. He could see the frown on her lips increasing. So he decided to change the subject.

"What do you say to hitting the water tomorrow?" He glanced over to the rushing water. "I'm in the mood to get wet."

"What?" she asked.

"Canoeing. You did say you liked to go?"

She nodded slowly. "Yes, but . . ."

"Good. I'll pick you up around eight tomorrow morning." He reached down and took her hand in his again and stood up, pulling her with him.

"Logan?"

He stopped all the questions by placing his lips over hers again. "Later." He smiled. "I'll take you home. I've got to go find all my gear in my uncle's garage. That is if we're going to hit the water tomorrow . . ."

She nodded.

◆　◆　◆

By the time he finally made it over to his uncle's house, it was after dark. He had a key to the place, but still chose to knock on the front door. When his uncle answered in a pair of basketball shorts and T-shirt, he knew he wouldn't get out of shooting some hoops with the older man before he could finally dig through the garage to get his canoe and paddles.

The man was an ox, except when it came to basketball. Then he was a short and heavy white version of Michael Jordan. Even Logan, who was easily half the man's age, couldn't keep up with him. After the first ten minutes, Logan felt his lungs start to burn. Fifteen minutes later, his back and thighs stung.

"I don't know how you do it," he wheezed out as he leaned his hands on his knees, more than forty minutes later. "I mean, you've got to be close to a hundred." He looked up at his uncle, who just laughed at him.

"You're just out of shape and slow." His uncle wasn't even winded.

"Okay, now that you've sufficiently beaten me, I've got to go hunt down my gear. I'm hitting the water with Amy tomorrow." He walked over and reached down to pull open the garage door they'd been playing in front of.

When he looked back, he watched his uncle's face sober. "Are you sure about what you're doing with that girl?"

Logan laughed. "You're one to talk." He'd done little else than think of Amy and the game they had been playing.

He flipped on the garage light and started looking through the mess of junk he'd stored in his uncle's garage almost a month ago.

"What do you mean?" His uncle was beside him.

He glanced at his uncle's face. "Leah? How long have you been seeing that one and keeping it a secret?"

His uncle removed his ball cap and wiped his forehead while avoiding eye contact.

"Yeah, thought so." Logan turned back to the mess in the garage. He spotted his canoe. Now all he needed was the paddle and life vest.

"It's complicated, son."

"What relationship isn't?" He moved a box and jumped a little when he heard a small noise come from under the pile.

"What's that? A rat?" His uncle reached over and took hold of a baseball bat that was leaning by the door.

"I don't think so. It yelped." Logan carefully moved a few items until he could see a dark shadow curled up on an old shirt of his in the bottom of a box. "Did you leave the garage door open in the last few days?"

"Shoot. Yes, it was open for a couple of days, but I closed it last night. Why?" his uncle asked from behind him.

"Because there's a dog curled up here and it looks to be in pretty bad shape."

"A dog?" His uncle moved to his side.

"You probably sealed him in when you shut the garage door."

"The poor thing." His uncle started to reach for the small animal.

"I'd hang on if I were you. Just to be safe. Do you have a flashlight?"

"Sure." His uncle rushed over to his toolbox and dug in the bottom drawer, then came back and shone it in the bottom of the box.

The dog couldn't have been older than a few weeks, and he was surprised to discover there were actually three of them in there.

He glanced around. "Do you have any meat in the house?"

"Meat?" His uncle frowned. "I've got some leftover steak."

"Perfect, go get it." Logan took the box from the pile and gently set it near the entrance of the garage to wait for his uncle to return.

"Here you go," his uncle said as he walked out the front door and then handed Logan the plate of meat. It was still pink in the middle and smelled wonderful.

"This will work. I'm betting mama isn't far away and is waiting for her chance to rescue them . . ." He set the plate down in front of the box and pulled his uncle over to sit on the front porch.

It took less than five minutes of listening to those pups cry for a small black dog to slowly come out of the brush near the side of the house. Her fur was so matted with mud, it was hard to tell what type of dog she was.

They watched her wolf down the steak, then jump into the box with her pups. They could hear the three pups sucking down their own meal.

"Poor things. I can't believe I locked them in here. I've been in and out of the garage a few times, but never knew about them or the mama."

"I'm going to try something." He stood up. "You hang back a bit, we don't want to spook her."

His uncle nodded and Logan made his way slowly toward the box.

When he got within a few feet, the mother's head popped up and he could hear a low growl. He smiled and started talking to her softly as he continued to move forward.

When he was within a few feet of the box, the mother laid her head down on the side of the box and he watched her tail thump every time he spoke. Ten minutes later, he sat with the dogs in his lap. It didn't take long for him to fall helplessly in love with them all. He wondered how he was going to persuade his landlord to let him keep the dogs.

♦ ♦ ♦

Amy sat on her sofa in her shorts and tank top and waited for the knock on her door. By a quarter past eight, she was beginning to wonder if Logan had decided to call the whole day off.

He'd known all along who she was and had been playing with her. Why? What did he mean when he said that she'd never understood him? They had talked briefly about it, but so far she still didn't know his reasons for acting like he hadn't known her. Nor had he asked her why she'd acted the same way to him. So many questions, yet the attraction was drawing her closer to him.

Just as she was thinking of a million reasons why it was a good thing he hadn't shown up, there was a brisk knock on her door.

Sighing, she got up and walked over. When she opened the door, she noticed he was a little winded.

"Sorry." He brushed a quick kiss on her lips before she had a chance to dodge him or say anything. "Daisy and her girls kept me up all night." He walked into the room without her invitation.

"Daisy?" She blinked a few times, images of exotic girls hanging all over Logan flashing through her mind.

"Yeah." He turned toward her and held up his cell phone. "I found her last night at my uncle's. Can you believe how cute they are? All three of the pups are girls! Can you imagine?"

She walked over and took the phone from his hands. Looking down at the image on the screen, she smiled. A small black dog with a white mark on her forehead looked up at the camera, while three little dark puppies hung on her tits having a meal.

"I named her Daisy, because the mark looks like one," Logan said.

"What are you going to do with them?" she asked, handing the phone back to him.

"Keep them."

"All of them?" she asked.

"Well, sure, at least until the pups are bigger. Besides, you can't break up a new family."

She walked over to him and kissed him on the cheek. "Where are they now?"

"I'm hoping my landlady doesn't get wind of them hiding in my bathroom. At least, until I can see if she'll make an exception to the no pets rule."

She thought about it. She had always wanted a dog and had actually spent time at the local shelter trying to pick one out. She had plenty of room and having the extra company would be an added bonus. "You can bring them over here." She wondered why she had such a soft spot for animals, and Logan.

"Really?" His eyes lit up.

She nodded. "I own this place and there's no rule against pets."

"I was hoping you'd say that." He walked back to the front door and opened it, then reached down and picked up a large box sitting just outside and carried it in.

"You brought them along?" She should have known she'd walked right into another one of his traps. "Of course you did."

But when she saw the dark head and brown eyes pop up from the box, she realized she didn't care.

"Oh, aren't you sweet?" She rushed over and picked up the mama. "And you smell so good." She snuggled her face into the soft fur as the dog tried to lick her everywhere.

"I gave her a bath last night. And they're all fed." He dropped a bag of dog food next to the box. "I'm going to get a vet appointment for them all later this week."

She smiled over at him as she picked up the smallest puppy.

Her eyes weren't even opened yet. "I bet these aren't even two weeks old."

"My uncle thinks Daisy had them in his garage last week sometime, when he left the door open for a couple of days. She must have come and gone for a while, but he locked her out overnight last night."

"Well, we can set them up in the spare room for now." She glanced down at the mama. "I've got some newspaper to lay down for her, until we know if she's trained."

"She is, at least she barked last night to be let out and didn't have any accidents all night."

"Good, then we should get along just fine."

They spent a few minutes setting the family up in her spare room, which doubled as a home office. She made sure to put anything of value up high enough that a dog bent on chewing couldn't get to it.

"Come on, let's hit the water." He took her hand and shut the door to the room, leaving the mama with a full bowl of food and water. Not to mention a pile of newspapers, just in case.

"I stopped off and got the racks this morning." He pointed toward his new SUV, where a two-person canoe was strapped to the top. "Course, I had to get the bike rack too." He nodded to the back rack, which was empty.

"I have one for my Jeep. There're so many extras you can buy for Jeeps." She sighed. "It's so hard not to go overboard."

"I'm a little jealous of the Jeep."

"Oh?" she said, as he opened the passenger door for her.

"Yeah, but I needed something clients would feel comfortable riding in, if needed."

"I never let anyone ride with me. Actually, it's against RMR policy."

"Yeah?" He shut her door, and when he got behind the wheel, he glanced at her. "Why?"

"A few years back, Carol—you've met her?" She waited until he nodded. "Well, she was taking an older man to a showing and was basically assaulted."

He stopped backing up and looked at her. "What happened?"

"Let's just say your uncle paid to have everyone take self-defense classes and we're all required to carry Tasers now."

"I remember a few years back hearing about the Realtor who was killed."

"It's a job that can easily turn bad. We're out there, for the most part, on our own, trusting that the people we are meeting are who they say they are. RMR does a great job screening clients, but"—she glanced out the window as they made their way up the canyon—"you just never know."

"Have you had any close calls?"

"Nope, I'm very cautious. Besides, I have my own added protection." She leaned closer to him. "I carry my nine millimeter." The gun always made her feel safer.

"I just bet it's pink."

"Wouldn't have it any other way." She held her chin up high. She was proud of her ability to protect herself.

"Okay, we'll have to go to the shooting range sometime to see who's a better shot," he said.

"You'll just lose again," she joked.

"Wanna bet?" He glanced over at her and she felt her heart skip.

CHAPTER
TEN

By the time they made it to the Clear Creek Whitewater Park, there were at least a dozen other people getting ready to get in the water. It was a popular drop-off spot. There were even shuttles you could ride to get back to your car once you were done.

"Ready for this?" He pulled out a bag that held two life vests and helmets. He knew the route was under a mile long, but the whitewater rafting was some of the most fun around. He could have taken her up to the mountains where the water was a little more unpredictable, but he didn't know her skill set, and to be honest with himself, it had been years since he'd been in the water himself.

"I was born for this." She reached in the back for the two paddles.

It took them a few minutes to get everything to the edge of the water. There was a small training class going on behind them in the calmer waters, but he carried the canoe up to where the course started.

He watched her strap on her helmet and vest, then discard her sandals and set them with all the other shoes. They hit the water a few minutes later, with her riding lead.

Four hours later, they had made the trek over a dozen times and were completely and wonderfully soaked to the bone. He couldn't remember laughing so much in his entire childhood. He kept trying to keep his eyes off the tight, wet tank top she was wearing. Not to mention her perfect breasts and nipples that looked absolutely delicious.

"What do you say to stopping for some lunch?" he asked, glancing over his shoulder at her. He was a little winded from carrying the canoe back up to his car.

"I could eat." She leaned against the door, taking a couple of deep breaths herself, causing his eyes to zero in and watch the slow movement of her breasts as her lungs expanded. "I'd forgotten how many different muscle groups it takes to do this." She rubbed her right shoulder, making him wish he could feel how soft her skin was under his hands.

"Just last night, my uncle was trying to convince me I was out of shape." He rolled his own shoulders, feeling the tightness there. "I'm beginning to believe him."

She laughed, the low sweet sound sending signals straight to his groin. "Now I remember why I haven't done this in a while."

He lifted the canoe back onto the rack with her help.

"How about grabbing some burgers?" he suggested.

He watched her eyes roll with delight. "Sounds perfect." She almost groaned, and he felt his body stiffen even more when his thoughts turned to getting her to make those noises for a whole different reason.

Luckily, they'd both brought changes of clothes. As Logan took off his swimming trunks in the restroom, he imagined Amy pulling off her wet tank top in the neighboring ladies' room.

◆　◆　◆

"So, why did you really move back to Golden?" Amy asked, leaning her elbows on the table as they waited for their burgers to be delivered.

"And don't tell me it was to help your uncle out. RMR is doing better than it was when I was hired a few years ago."

He shut his mouth. "Fair enough." His mind raced to come up with something that didn't sound too desperate. The fact was that he'd worked himself into a corner. He had needed to make a change in his life, and upon hearing that she worked for his uncle, it had given him the perfect opportunity to set things straight with her. One of the last items on his life's list of things to correct. "I guess it was just time. Things were coasting along at CCR, but . . ." He leaned back in his chair and crossed his arms over his chest, reminded again of how sore they were. It felt great, though. "I mean, some of my best memories were in Golden. Now that my dad's gone . . ."

"Oh, I didn't know your father had passed." She frowned.

"Just before Christmas."

"I'm sorry," she replied.

He shrugged. "The old man and I were never really close. Actually, he's the reason my mom and my uncle went their separate ways."

"What happened?" She tilted her head and waited.

"My uncle never really approved of my father. Kevin, my dad, was a military brat, and after spending a few years in the Corps, he thought he knew how he should raise his son . . . by using an iron fist." He closed his eyes, he could still feel the belt as it landed across his backside.

"I'm sorry." She leaned toward him in her chair, her hand reached for his.

"I guess it's one of the reasons why I was so wild in my youth," he suggested.

"So, you admit it." Her eyebrows went up and a light smile played on her lips.

He glanced at her in question.

She smiled fully. "That you were a rascal."

He raised his hand in defeat. "I blame it solely on my old man."

"It wasn't your father who threw a string of lit firecrackers in the girls' dressing room, hoping, no doubt, that we'd all run out half dressed."

"Imagine my dismay when Mrs. Kaiser came out with the bottom of her sweats burned instead."

They laughed until their meals were delivered.

"What about your folks?" He glanced at her once he'd wolfed down half of his burger.

"They're both still alive."

"Didn't they divorce a long time ago?"

"Yes, but for some reason, they recently started trying to make it work . . . they've actually started going out on dates again. It's kind of embarrassing now that they've started acting like teenagers around one another."

"Maybe divorce works for them?" He'd never imagined that his own parents' relationship would have lasted as long as it had.

"When they were married, they fought all the time. Now, not so much. Besides, if they start to drive each other crazy, they just go back to their own places."

"I'm not sure I could ever have a real relationship like that."

"Agreed. It is better than Kristen's parents, though, who seem to go out of their way to touch each other and kiss every time people are around."

"Too much PDA?" he asked.

"Kristen is always complaining about it."

"Kristen?" He tried to remember whom she was talking about. Then an image of a cheery, honey-haired girl who had always been beside Amy popped into his mind. "Your best friend from school?"

She nodded and took another bite of her burger.

"What's she up to?"

"She works at an architectural firm in downtown Denver as an interior designer. She's been engaged for a couple of years, but her big day is coming up." She pushed her plate away. "We're finally going to pick out her wedding dress next weekend."

He didn't get where he was today without knowing when it was a good time to change the subject. And, seeing her eyes mist up now, he knew there was no better time to talk about something else.

"So, what's up between my uncle and Leah?" he asked.

He thought he heard her chuckle at the change of subject, but then she leaned forward and started telling him when she'd first walked in on them together.

Not that Logan was afraid of marriage talk, but since the last time he'd almost gone down that road himself and had ended up losing a small chunk of his heart, he liked avoiding thoughts of marriage whenever possible.

In the back of his mind, he kept wondering how his prior engagement would have turned out differently had his fiancée been Amy instead of Bella.

◆ ◆ ◆

When Logan pulled the car up in front of her townhouse, nerves flew through her. She didn't know why. After all it was Sunday afternoon, the sun was still warm and bright, and it wasn't like they'd been on a romantic date, like the night before when he'd walked her to the door and kissed her softly before getting back in his car and driving away.

This time, however, she doubted he'd leave after just a quick kiss. Nor did she really want him to. She'd had fun today. And after talking with him over the last few days, she was beginning to see just how much he'd really changed.

Not only was she enjoying herself with him, she was finding it harder to deny the attraction she felt for him. Every time she found him looking at her, she would almost melt from the heat in his eyes.

"I'd like to check on the family." He glanced at her plaintively.

"Oh, yes." She remembered that she now had a room full of dogs to care for. "Come on in."

He jumped out and rushed around to open her door. She took a couple of deep breaths and tried to steady herself as she waited.

As they walked into her townhouse, they heard soft barking.

"Sounds like Daisy needs out." He went past her and opened the door. The small, dark dog darted through his legs, past her, and out the open door.

"Will she come back on her own?"

"As long as the pups are here, you shouldn't worry about her going too far."

She waited with the front door open while the dog did her business in her small front yard area. Logan had disappeared into her guest room, and she could hear the puppies yapping as he no doubt played with them.

When Daisy came rushing back in, Amy shut the door and followed the new mother back into the makeshift nursery.

"How are they?" She walked over and looked into the box and watched the pups start suckling on their mom.

"Great. I can't thank you enough for letting them stay here for a while." He brushed his hand over Daisy's head. Instantly, Amy felt a wave of desire slam into her. She wondered what it would feel like if he touched *her* with such tenderness.

"Do you want a drink?" She walked back to the doorway of the room. His eyes traveled over her and then his smile took her breath away. Could he tell that she was almost shaking as he watched her?

He followed her into her living room just as she started to pour some lemonade. She jumped when his large hands spanned her waist and spun her around.

"I'd rather have something else," he said softly. Then dipped his head toward hers and brushed his lips against hers. Her fingers dug into his hair, holding him to her mouth a moment longer as a moan of pleasure escaped her.

"This is what I've craved all day." His fingers dug into her hips as he moved closer, pinning her against her countertop.

She could feel his legs move in between hers and gladly spread her feet so he could get closer. Then, he moved his hands until he was lifting her to the edge of the counter. Her legs wrapped around his narrow hips, his mouth never leaving hers as his tongue darted in to mix with her own. She threw her head back as his lips trailed down her neck, lapping at every nerve along the way. She couldn't stop her body from wanting, from moving against his.

"Tell me to leave." He moaned against her skin, his hands brushing the sides of her breasts, sending a shiver up her spine.

She was beyond control and could only shake her head slightly as she ran her fingers over his arms, his chest. Why would she tell him that? What she wanted was for him to carry her into her bedroom and . . .

Just then, her doorbell sounded off in three quick bursts. Kristen. Damn!

Logan glanced up at her, his sandy eyebrows shooting up in question.

"Anyone you can get rid of in under a minute?"

She leaned her head back against the cabinet. "Nope."

He groaned, then ran his mouth over hers one more time. "Okay, give me a minute." He took a couple of deep breaths and she stifled a giggle. She needed a few minutes herself.

When she opened her door, Kristen was hidden behind a pile of magazines. "I need your help!" She pushed past Amy but stopped dead in the middle of her living room when she saw Logan leaning against her bar area.

"Oh!" She glanced between them and a slow smile crossed her lips. "I hope I'm not interrupting anything."

"You are," Logan said, under his breath.

"No!" Amy said quickly and a little more loudly than she should have.

Logan crossed his arms over his chest. Amy couldn't stop her eyes from roaming over the muscles she'd been running her hands over a moment ago.

"I'll just—" Kristen started.

"No!" Amy broke in. "We had plans." She reached over and took some of the magazines from her friend. She glanced toward Logan, who just smiled back at her. "I promised Kristen I'd look through these in preparation for our bridal shop appointments next weekend."

Daisy came into the room and Kristen gasped. "You have a dog!" She quickly set the rest of the magazines in a messy pile on Amy's coffee table, then rushed over and picked up Daisy.

"Well, Logan has a dog. I'm watching her and her puppies until—"

"Puppies?" Kristen broke in, then rushed with Daisy into the spare room. Logan walked up behind Amy and placed his hands on her hips as they listened to Kristen *ooh* and *aah* over the dogs.

He turned her using his hands on her hips. "I'd better let you two have some time." He stepped closer to her and she felt her body instantly respond. "I'll see you in the morning." He leaned down and kissed her until she felt her toes start to curl.

"Later." She knew she'd have a lot of explaining to do with Kristen after he left.

No sooner had the front door closed, than Kristen was by her side, hands at her hips, her head tilted questioningly. "Spill!"

Amy thought she saw a slight smile on her friend's lips. Closing her eyes, she tried to calm her body down from the onslaught that was Logan Miller.

CHAPTER
ELEVEN

All next week Logan found it hard to concentrate every time she was within his sight. He took to using his uncle's office, since he had a full schedule that week and was hardly there.

Amy kept getting more lovely every time he'd seen her. Monday, she'd worn a sexy cream-colored dress, which had hugged every curve. The deep *V* ran off her shoulders, dipping low over those breasts he'd gotten his hands on just the day before. She'd worn heels, making her the same height as him. He found the ensemble so damn sexy that he had wanted to pull her into a closet or empty office somewhere to see how quickly he could discard her entire outfit.

That's when he'd decided he needed to use his uncle's office for the day. Of course, Tuesday had come along and this time it had been a gray skirt, with a deep-red, off-the-shoulder blouse. She'd covered the blouse with a blazer that matched the skirt, but the second she'd removed it, he'd hightailed it to his uncle's office to hide behind the desk for the remainder of the day.

Then on Wednesday, they'd been called out to another meeting with the McCormack Group to finalize their offer. Her outfit that day had definitely been his undoing. The entire twenty minutes they sat around the boardroom table, the men in the meeting couldn't stop staring at her cleavage as the curve of her breasts threatened to peek out of the crisp white blouse. He caught himself growling a warning to the other men.

When they were walking back to his car that evening, he pulled her into his arms and kissed her as he ran his hands over every inch of the tan skirt. Reluctant to release her, he nevertheless dropped his arms and opened the door for her.

Her eyes were unfocused, her hair was a little messed up, and the back of her shirt had come untucked from the skirt. He couldn't stop himself from smiling as she righted herself while he drove back toward their office.

"Do you always dress like this?" He watched her glide pink lip gloss over her bottom lip. Just the simple movement alone was causing his pants to become too tight.

"Like what?" she asked.

"You still carrying that gun of yours?"

She frowned even more. "Always." She tapped her purse that sat next to her. "Why?"

"How about the Taser?"

She nodded.

"You might need it later."

When they entered the office building, it was to pounding rain and thunder. He usually loved the summer storms, but this one seemed to only build his mood even more. He felt the air between Amy and him crackle as they stepped into the elevator.

When the doors slid closed he was shocked when she swooped over and pushed him up against the elevator wall. Her glossed lips glided over his, her sweet scent filled his senses as her hands ran over his arms and chest. She'd pushed herself up against him, and he knew he'd be walking funny into his uncle's office once the doors opened again.

"Tell me that was your last meeting for the day," he said against her skin as his hands pushed up her skirt so he could feel her bare skin under his fingers.

"All done for the day," she purred.

"Then why in God's name are we going back to the office?" He reached over and hit the lobby button as the car came to a halt on the second floor.

She giggled and leaned back as the doors slid open. He was thankful no one was in the hallway, and even more thankful that no one would be riding back down with them.

The second the doors closed, she was back on him, pushing him a little harder against the wall this time as she took his mouth with hers.

"You're in so much trouble," he growled as he felt her hike up her skirt to wrap a leg around his calf.

"Promise?" she teased.

His eyes closed as he ran his hands over her hips. "My place is closer."

"Don't make me wait too long."

When they walked out of the building's lobby, her skirt was twisted sideways. Her hair was messy again from his hands, and her newly applied lip gloss was coating his own lips and face.

His tie was completely loose so he pulled it off as he held open his car door for Amy, then shoved it into his jacket pocket. Wondering how fast he could get to his apartment, he tried not to focus on the way she crossed her legs on the short ride.

When they finally pulled into his covered parking spot at the apartment complex, he wasted no time and pulled her into his lap. A hard task, since there was a large console between their seats. She quickly maneuvered her skirt over her hips, causing his blood to boil.

His hands went to her smooth legs as her mouth fused to his. Her fingers ran through his hair, then traveled down his neck before settling on his shoulders and arms.

He heard her moan when he reached up between her soft thighs and pulled the silk material aside to finally run his finger over the softest skin he'd ever had the pleasure of feeling.

"Logan." She leaned back and bit her bottom lip as her eyes closed. His finger dipped into her slickness and he watched her hips jolt a little.

He could watch her all day like this. The way her light eyelashes rested on her pink cheeks. Her hair was completely messed up, and he loved her disheveled look. Her shirt was coming unbuttoned, thanks to his own hands, giving him a view of silk, lace, and soft, pale skin underneath.

Reaching up with his free hand, he unbuttoned until he could tug her breast free from her bra and run his mouth over her erect nipple. Her hands tightened in his hair and he felt her breath hitch.

"Yes, that's it." He moaned against her skin. He wanted to feel her lose control. Here. Now. His fingers explored her deeper and he felt her hips start to move with each slide of his own. She was rubbing her thighs against his erection still contained in his slacks. Which was only causing him pleasure. His eyes were glued to her face as he watched her skin heat. He bent forward to lick his way around her exposed breasts again.

"That's it, come undone for me." He quickened his pace and watched her flush as she exploded around his fingers. He'd never experienced anything so wonderful in his life.

She melted down onto his chest, her head resting on his shoulder as he felt her body relax. He knew he wasn't done with her, not by a long shot, but for phase two, he needed to get them up three flights of stairs.

Sighing, he started to button up her shirt, but got only one done. Then he reached into the back seat where he'd thrown his blazer and wrapped it around her instead.

She looked down at him. "I must look a mess." She reached for her hair, but he took her wrists and stopped her.

"No, don't change a thing. I want you just the way you are, in my bed." He quickly opened the door. She grabbed her heels, which he hadn't known she'd discarded before climbing over the console.

Then he watched her slip them on and felt himself twitch at the thought of her in his bed with nothing but the sexy shoes on.

"What?" She frowned down at him.

He shook his head, not trusting the words that would come out of his mouth if he spoke. Spanning her waist with his hands, he set her outside his door on the concrete and then grabbed his keys and followed her. Taking her hand, he rushed them up the stairs and felt a little winded when he finally reached his doorway.

He heard her giggle and catch her own breath when he shoved his key into the lock.

◆　◆　◆

"Logan," she started to say, but he pulled her inside quickly, removed the blazer, and then pushed her back up against his door. His mouth covered hers again. His hands went to her hips, hiking her skirt high, until her panties were completely exposed.

"God help me, I want you so bad," he groaned against her mouth.

She'd never experienced anything like what he'd done to her in the car. Nor had she ever felt so exposed. Actually, making out in a car was one teenage experience she'd avoided in her youth.

Now, as an adult, she could totally appreciate the whimsy of it all and the excitement. His finger found her heated, swollen skin and started playing across its slickness. She felt her knees almost give out, and if it hadn't been for his body pressed up against hers and the door, she would have melted to the floor.

Then, he was on his knees, his hands pulling her panties down over her shoes as his mouth touched her, his tongue dipping deep inside her as she cried out his name.

Her fingers went to his hair, holding him, directing him over her flesh. She realized she was begging as both his tongue and one finger dipped inside her to pleasure her.

"Please." She moaned when she felt herself building fast. "Logan, I need . . ."

"What?" He stood quickly, then lifted her in his arms. "Tell me what you need," he growled as he walked fast toward the back of his apartment.

Her eyes met his silver ones and she felt her heart skip a little. "You." It came out as a whisper.

His smile was fast as he laid her gently on his bed. Her eyes were glued to him. She watched as he removed his shirt, a little too slowly. She wanted to reach up and rip the buttons off but felt like she was frozen in place. Finally, he tossed the shirt into a corner and put his hands on his belt. She sat up and covered his hands with her own.

"Let me," she said, throwing the belt over to the same corner. His hands had dropped to his sides, his eyes watching her face closely. When she slowly ran her hand over his hardness, still tucked inside his slacks, he moaned and closed his eyes, his head falling back. She did this a few more times, before slowly sliding his zipper down and releasing him fully.

He was beautiful. Of course, no man liked to hear that word used to describe him, but there was no other word that would have done the moment justice. She tugged his slacks until they pooled around his feet. When he stepped out of them, he frowned.

"How is it that I'm naked and you still have all of your clothes on?" He smiled. "Looks like it's my turn." He reached for her shirt.

"I'm not wearing any panties." She scooted farther onto the bed.

"Yes." He ran his tongue over his lips and groaned. "I remember now."

He got onto his knees on the edge of the bed and crawled closer to her. His hands reached out and took her by the hips, holding her still. When she stopped edging away, she watched his fingers undo the remaining button of her blouse.

"Do you realize how crazy you made every man in that board-room today?" His eyes went to hers and they grew dark with desire. "This . . ." He ran a finger lightly over the crest of her breast. Her head rolled back, and she felt her breath hitch as her heart raced. "I couldn't keep my eyes off of this part." He dipped his head and ran his mouth over the same spot.

His fingers pushed the light material off her shoulders. She felt him reach around her and unclasp her bra and moved to help him remove it.

"Let me . . ." he said against her skin. "Let me take care of you."

When she was finally exposed, he leaned back and looked at her. She thought she heard him whisper, "Perfect." But couldn't be sure, since her heart was beating too loudly in her ears for her to hear.

Then he ran the back of his fingers over her lightly, she closed her eyes, and then she could no longer see either.

"Please," she begged again. He was making her body heat and all she wanted was to be next to him, skin against skin.

She opened her eyes again. He'd moved to the edge of the bed and was using his hands to pull down her skirt. She was still wearing her heels and she reached down to remove them.

"No, leave them." He smiled as he tossed her skirt into the same corner. Then he was moving back up the mattress to settle between her spread legs. Her knees were bent and her heels rested on the soft bed.

His hands ran up her legs, pushing them higher as he moved closer to her. She watched him open a condom and roll it on his full length. Just the simple act had her insides clenching with desire.

She'd never wanted someone as much as she wanted him. His eyes moved to hers and the edges of his mouth curved up. How had she never realized just how sexy his smile was before? She'd always seen it as annoying because usually he had been laughing at her. Now, however, his mouth looked too good to ignore.

When he leaned closer, her eyes followed the movement until she felt those lips on hers again. His hand was still resting on her outer thigh and when he moved against her, she moaned and raised her hips to meet him. He rubbed against the tender skin where she wanted him to fill her.

"Yes. I love those little noises you make," he said as his mouth traveled down her neck.

"You're driving me crazy." She gripped his hips, trying to get him to move where she wanted him.

"Now you know how I felt all day. Imagine sitting across the table with this all during that meeting." He rubbed his full length against her in one quick slide.

She arched and groaned, the image of how he'd looked as they'd sat in the staff boardroom flashed in her mind. Then it was replaced with how he looked now. Hovering above her, naked, erect.

Her legs wrapped around his hips, her heels pressed up against his thighs.

"Yes," he groaned as he moved closer. "Do you feel it?"

She met his eyes as he slid quickly into her.

CHAPTER TWELVE

Logan could have easily died at that very moment and he would have died a happy man. Amy's hair was fanned out over his shoulder and chest and he could feel her skin start to cool next to his.

He was running his fingers through her hair slowly, enjoying the softness of it as he felt his own heart rate settle down.

"What do you say to ordering some pizza and spending the rest of the evening here?"

She lifted her head and looked at him. "What do you say to grabbing Chinese as you drive me home so we won't leave Daisy locked up all night without a bathroom break?"

In all his desire, he'd forgotten about the little dogs. "I guess my mind was focused on keeping you in bed all night." He sat up, then dressed in an old pair of jeans. As he was pulling a sweatshirt over his head, he heard the crash of thunder and glanced toward his windows.

Finally, the skies had opened up and rain was pelting everything outside. He frowned when he noticed her buttoning up her blouse.

It was a little wrinkled, and when he noticed her skirt was as well, he couldn't stop from smiling.

"I've got some old sweats . . ." he started to say, but she just shook her head.

"I'm fine." She finished buttoning her shirt.

"Okay, but at least wear this." He handed her his rain jacket. "It's coming down in buckets now."

She looked out his window, then took the coat.

They made a dash for the carport, both of them laughing. As he jumped in behind the wheel he watched her shake the jacket off before entering his car.

"Where is there a good Chinese place?"

"A block from my townhouse. If you drop me off at my Jeep, you can follow."

He reached over and brushed her hair behind her shoulder. She'd disappeared into his bathroom for a few minutes and had emerged without a single hair out of place. He'd just have to enjoy messing her up again.

He supposed dropping her off at her own car made sense, but something inside him didn't want a moment away from her. When they finally made it back to her place, it was after dark.

The second she opened her front door, Daisy rushed between his legs, happy to see them both, then quickly went and did her business.

"She's really quite a great dog," Amy said, setting her bag down on the bar.

He set the take-out down on the kitchen table, then laughed when Daisy sat down and glanced at the boxes.

"She loves human food. I know you're not supposed to give them much, but I cooked her eggs and rice the other morning."

"I bet she'll really enjoy some of this then." He held up the box of white rice. "I'm sure a little can't hurt. After all, she's eating for four."

They sat on the sofa and watched television while they ate, then he carried Amy into her bedroom. He slowly peeled off her skirt and shirt. And when he got her completely naked, and she was calling out his name, he knew he wanted to keep her that way until morning.

◆ ◆ ◆

Amy woke with a start when something brushed against her face. When she opened her eyes, she was looking directly into silver ones as Logan was smiling down at her. She could tell by the darkness of the room that she had plenty of time before they were due into the office.

"You're a hard person to wake," he said. "Daisy and I have been trying for a while now."

As if on cue, the small dog stuck her face between theirs and started kissing Amy. It took awhile to recover from laughing as she tried to shove both Logan and Daisy off her face, since he had joined in the excitement.

"I like this side of you," Logan said after the small dog jumped off the bed to return to her crying pups.

"Which side?" She desperately wished she could retreat to the bathroom to freshen up, but since Logan was holding her down, she doubted she'd get a chance just yet.

"The messy side. Your hair's all around your face." He released one of her hands and used a finger to push a strand away from her face. "Your face is clear of makeup." He leaned down and placed a kiss on her lips. "And, the best part of it is," he said as he glanced down at her, "your clothes are nowhere to be found."

She moaned as he leaned down and started kissing her again. She could get used to being woken up like this. He still held her arms above her head with his free hand and she wished she could touch him, since he, too, was naked.

He had a body that she doubted she would ever tire of running her hands over. When he finally released her hands, she grabbed hold of him and didn't let go until he was moaning.

She reversed their positions and held his hands above his head. He could have broken loose if he'd tried, but instead he just looked up at her.

"Getting back at me?" he asked.

She felt her heart skip, and to answer him, she leaned down and ran her mouth over his neck and chest slowly. When she felt him try to break free, she stopped him by putting her hands on his chest.

"No, it's my turn to take care of you," she said against his skin as she ran her mouth lower, over very impressive six-pack abs, downward, until she followed a small patch of brown hair that led her to his sex.

When she used her mouth on him, his hands went into her hair, gripping her as she enjoyed every inch of him.

She felt herself growing hotter, wanting him deep inside her, and as she crawled back up to straddle him, he handed her a condom. She slowly rolled it on him and watched his eyes close with pleasure.

"Watch me," she said, hovering above him. "Watch." She didn't know what made her say it, but his eyes darkened as he watched her slide inch by inch on his length. His fingers dug into her soft hips as she moved above him. When he pushed her to go faster, she was right there with him, beat for beat.

When she finally felt herself explode, he wrapped his arms around her waist and growled her name into her hair.

Once her skin had cooled, she shivered and reached for the blankets.

"Oh, no you don't. It's time to get up." He ran his hand over her naked bottom, then slapped it lightly. "I'm hungry and since I've been up for a while, I know there's nothing in that fridge of yours."

"Keeps me from eating too much."

He rolled out from under her and hopped out of bed. Instead of waiting for her to do the same, he picked her up and started carrying her into the bathroom as she giggled. He turned on the shower, and by the time the water was warm, he had her moaning again.

She'd never dressed as quickly as she did that morning. She normally took almost an hour and a half each morning to put herself together, but under Logan's watchful eye, she sped up to just forty minutes.

Her long hair hung freely, still wet in places, as she pulled out of her parking spot and glanced in the rearview mirror to make sure he was following her to one of her favorite breakfast spots.

She knew he still needed to swing by his place and dress for the office, so when they entered Café 20, she walked up to the counter and ordered the fastest breakfast sandwich while he drooled over the donuts.

"I don't know how you expect to stay in shape, eating those," she said as they sat down. He'd set a plate of three donuts and a ham breakfast sandwich in front of him.

"I worked up an appetite this morning." He smiled over at her as he held up the chocolate glazed donut for her. "Go ahead, I won't tell. Besides, one couldn't hurt."

"With me, it's never just one."

His eyes stayed on hers as he licked the chocolate from the donut.

Her face flushed and she felt herself grow hotter as he watched her.

She was never more aware of being watched than she had been that morning. The sensation had done nothing but make her wish they could have taken the day off and spent the time in her bed instead.

"How do you expect me to concentrate on work today while you're dressed like that?" He glanced over at her simple black skirt and burgundy top.

"How would you notice? You've been hiding in your uncle's office all week anyway."

He frowned. "For my own good," he said as they walked out of the café. Then he took her hand and tugged her to a stop before she could open the Jeep's door. "I'm not sure I can handle working in the same room with you, knowing now what you look like under those clothes."

She wrapped her arms around his neck. "And you think I'm not feeling the same?" Her eyes ran up and down him slowly. "I suppose we'll just have to suffer together." He leaned down and kissed her softly.

When she walked into the office a few minutes later, she had eight voice mail messages on her phone.

She patiently listened to them all as she tried not to wonder how long it would take Logan to go home, change his clothes, and come walking through her door. She marked down on her calendar the new listings for the rest of the week, not to mention the open house that was planned for the end of the month, as well as the big Denver Metro Realtor Association party that was held once a year in early September. She vaguely wondered if Logan would take her and what she'd wear. Then she noticed that she'd marked off all day this Saturday on her calendar to go wedding dress shopping with Kristen, and her heart jumped with excitement. She'd been waiting for this day her entire life and knew that Kristen had been as well.

She spent the next few minutes remembering how often they had talked about the day they would get married. What they would wear, how they would style their hair, so many details, but never once had they described their perfect man.

For as long as Amy had thought about it, the only detail she was one hundred percent clear on was that she would never marry anyone like Logan Miller. She chuckled just as her office door opened and Logan stepped in.

"Something funny?" He walked over and stopped on the other side of her desk. He looked extremely handsome today in a dark gray suit. His hair was combed back and he'd taken the time to shave.

Instantly she felt her face flush. "No, nothing."

"Oh, really?" He leaned his hip on the edge of her desk, looking quite amused. Just looking into his silver eyes made her heart skip as she remembered how they looked when he was above her, inside of her.

"Now *that* look I know." His smile grew as he whispered to her. "I can't wait to see that look again tonight."

She blushed, just as his uncle walked through her office door.

"There you are, my boy, come on, grab your stuff, I'm taking you to my next meeting."

Instantly, Amy's guard went up. She stood slowly. "Your meeting with Fowler and Fowler?"

Gary nodded. "Yeah, I'm getting tired of running around in circles with this couple." He turned back toward Logan. "Just because a couple of lawyers got married and went into business together doesn't mean that they know anything about purchasing a building for their new law firm."

Amy felt a wave of jealousy rush through her. She'd initially asked to take part in that transaction and here he was taking Logan. No doubt, all because they were related.

Logan smiled and slapped his uncle on the back. "Need a little mediation, huh?" They both chuckled as they walked out of her office without another word.

As she sat back down, she could no longer deny that maybe Gary was really getting ready to hand RMR over to Logan.

Had he known this piece of information all along? Doubt filled her mind as she prepared herself for her first showing of the day. Thursdays and Fridays were usually her busiest days for showings.

When she drove up to the property less than twenty minutes later, her client was already waiting by the front door. The house, situated along a busy road, had sat empty for the last two months and had had only a handful of viewings. She was really hoping for an offer soon.

"Morning," she called out as she stepped out of her Jeep. The younger man nodded toward her. He was built like a linebacker but easily her age or younger. Instantly she was on guard. She didn't like going on showings when the client was a single man.

Taking out her phone, she texted Ana, the office manager.

SM showing ok

Which let the office know that she was showing a listing to a single male. She would text again when she was done with the showing. If the office didn't hear back from her in half an hour, Ana would call the police to that location and give them the client's information.

Ana's message came back quickly. *SM Info rcvd for Chris Hough*

"Chris?" Amy smiled as she walked toward the man.

"Uh, yeah." He held out his hand; she took it easily.

"I'm Amy Walker." He dropped his hand and shoved it in his jeans. "So, what exactly are you looking for?" She liked to get an idea before she showed anyone the inside of a place.

"Well, uh." He glanced around, taking in the busy street. "It's really for my dad. He's getting older and," he looked across the street, "I saw this place was close to the fire station."

She looked across the street where the firehouse sat farther down the road. There was even an ambulance station next door.

"The hospital is only a few blocks away," she hinted.

"Yeah." He looked relieved. "Dad's been fighting cancer for a few years now."

"Oh, I'm sorry to hear that." She felt herself start to relax.

"Well, he's in remission now, but I'd like to get him moved closer to me." He shrugged. "I'm on the School of Mines campus."

"Oh?" she asked. "Do you go there?"

"No, I teach there." His chest puffed. "Graduated last year with my PhD and they brought me on as faculty a few months ago."

"Wow." She tilted her head toward him. "I'm thoroughly impressed."

He smiled, and for the first time she saw a softer side of the man.

She was reminded of how she'd misjudged Logan and his intentions recently, about his past and possibly the reasons he'd acted out so much as a child. She didn't feel like she was one to judge someone so quickly, but maybe she was off her game lately.

"Well, let me show you around." She opened the door and let him walk in first.

CHAPTER
THIRTEEN

By the time Logan made it back to the office, it was after lunch. His uncle had insisted that they go out for Mexican food. He couldn't just tell his uncle that he wanted to spend the day with Amy, so he'd let himself be dragged around from meeting to meeting.

When he entered Amy's office, he frowned when he saw it was empty. He walked over to her desk and flipped through her calendar, noticing that she had been booked with showings all day and would even be out most of tomorrow. He went out to the main reception area and stopped in front Ana's desk, the woman in charge of scheduling.

"Is Amy out of town on a listing?"

She glanced up at him. "Let me look." She punched her keyboard then looked back at him. "No, she's in town today, she should be at this property now." She wrote the address down on a piece of paper. "I'm sure she's still there."

"Thanks." He took the paper and walked out to see if he could still catch her.

It took him less than ten minutes before he pulled in front of the larger home that took up most of the hillside. Since it was gated, he looked back down at the slip of paper and was happy to see that Ana had included the entry code next to the address.

He pulled up and stopped next to Amy's Jeep. The stone house was gorgeous and easily worth a couple of million. After talking with his uncle, he was convinced that RMR's higher listings were all thanks to the direction Amy had taken the agency. Before, his uncle sold only a few homes a year worth more than half a million. Last year alone, they had sold close to three dozen and he didn't think it had anything to do with the booming economy.

When he stepped inside the massive front doors, he called out into the empty space and waited for a response. When he was met with silence, he frowned. As he started walking around the main floor, terrible images flooded his mind.

He kept calling her name over and over again. Just when he was about to start running through the house, screaming her name, he spotted her standing out back with an older couple.

Taking several deep breaths, he tried to stop his hands from shaking. When he walked out the glass patio doors, he pasted on a smile and approached the group.

"Hi," he called out. Amy turned slightly away from the couple. She was wearing a dark pair of sunglasses and he wished more than anything he could have seen her eyes as he walked toward her.

"Mr. and Mrs. Pennington, this is Logan Miller, Gary's nephew."

"Oh, how do you do? We simply adore your uncle." The woman reached out her hand and took his.

"I hope you don't mind, I was just in the neighborhood and wanted to see this place." He whistled and glanced around. "What a view."

"Yes, we were just admiring it ourselves," the man said, wrapping his arm around his wife. Instantly Logan felt a wave of something flood him. In his mind, he could just imagine Amy and himself standing in the same spot thirty years from now.

They made small talk for a while, then he stood back and let Amy finish the deal. By the time the older couple left, she had a signed offer in her hands.

He watched the gate on the house close, then pulled her into his arms. When he felt her tense he turned her around and gently removed her sunglasses so he could see into those blue eyes of hers.

"Regret already?" He frowned, not wanting to let her go.

Her eyes avoided his as she shook her head slightly. "No."

"Then?" He waited, and when she wouldn't meet his gaze, he used his fingers to lift her chin until she looked at him. "Why the stiffness?"

"It's nothing." Her arms wrapped around his shoulders and she leaned closer to him.

"Amy, if I've done . . ."

"No," she interrupted him. "It's nothing. Really." She smiled at him and he could see she was struggling with a decision.

"You can tell me, you know." He waited until she nodded her head, then he dipped his head and tasted her lips. "I've been thinking about this all day."

"As have I." Her fingers went to his hair. "You know, the Penningtons were my last showing for the day."

"Hmm?" His eyebrows rose in desire.

"We do have this big, empty house all to ourselves." She stretched out her words as a smile spread on her lips.

"Tell me there's a bed or a sofa left in this place."

"No, but there's this really solid countertop in the kitchen."

He growled and started pulling her in the direction he'd remembered seeing the large kitchen. Huge windows overlooked the backyard and view, but he didn't stop to enjoy them. Instead, he backed her up until her hips hit the marble, then he hoisted her until she sat on the edge of the smooth surface.

His mouth met hers as her hands pushed his shirt off his shoulders and his hands removed her silk panties in one quick swipe, ripping them at the hip. She gasped, then giggled nervously until his fingers found her, swollen and wet for him.

"Tell me you've wanted this all day." He groaned against her skin. When she nodded her head, his lips rained kisses across her exposed neck while his fingers dipped inside her heat. Her hips jerked closer to him as her head fell backward. Her moan matched his when he lowered his body, grabbed her thighs, and leaned them on his shoulders. He replaced his fingers with his mouth. When he tasted her arousal, he almost came undone.

She was sweeter than anything he'd ever tasted before. Her pink flesh called to him as he lapped at her while her sexy heels dug into his shoulders. She was leaning back, her head resting against the cabinets as he licked her to completion.

Then, he was sheathing himself and sliding into her before she could make a full recovery. Her eyes opened on a groan as he filled her. Their movements synchronized. His hips rushing faster and faster until he felt her convulse around him again, only then did he allow himself to fall with her.

♦ ♦ ♦

Amy couldn't believe what had just happened. She was lying on the carpeted floor in a four million dollar home completely naked with Logan sprawled on top of her.

She giggled. "How long do you think it would take us to do that in every room in a house this size?"

He leaned up on his elbows and looked down at her. "First off, I'd have to have food. Second, a box of condoms, third"—he bent down and kissed her before saying—"at least a sofa or chair once in a while. I'm sure we're both going to have rug burns in places we'd rather not mention." He groaned as he rolled off her. "It is a great house."

"It's too big."

He laughed. "Right."

"No." She rolled toward him, her fingers played with the light dusting of hair on his chest. "It is. I don't know what a couple the age of the Penningtons is going to do with a place like this."

"Probably the same thing we just spent two hours doing."

"Yeah, right."

"I don't know," he said as his hand went to her hip, holding her close. "Did you see the way Mr. Pennington was running his hands over Mrs. Pennington?"

She couldn't help it, she laughed until her stomach growled.

"Okay, on one point we agree. We need food."

"Now, where did we leave our clothes?" He looked around.

A little over an hour later, they pulled in front of a restaurant in his car, after dropping her Jeep off at her townhouse and letting Daisy out for a much-needed potty break.

"Didn't this used to be a Laundromat?" he asked.

"Yeah, wait until you see what they did to it now." She raced up and opened the doors for him. He stepped inside.

"Wow." He shook his head. "Doesn't look like a Laundromat now."

The family-run Italian restaurant was one of her favorite spots in Golden. It was small enough that it felt homey, but big enough that there was still room for forty tables. Most of which sat out on a back patio during the warmer months.

"Shall we dine outside?" She pointed toward the back doors. "It's 'seat yourself' here."

"Sounds nice." He followed her to one of her favorite tables. She sat in her usual spot. She couldn't hold back a smile as she watched him sit in the chair next to her, instead of across the table.

"So, what's good here?" He glanced at the paper menus that sat on the table.

"Everything." She felt her stomach growl. "But I especially like the calzones." She heard his stomach rumble. "I think yours has already made up its mind for you." She chuckled as he laughed.

"My stomach and I are in your capable hands."

After she ordered a bottle of wine and calzones for the both of them, they sat and sipped their drinks as the sun set over the mountains. String lights hung above their heads as soft music played in the background.

She couldn't have picked a more perfect ending to a night if she'd wanted to.

"So," he leaned closer to her after she'd pushed her almost empty plate aside, "now that we've had food, I'll bet we can find a bed somewhere."

"It's really a shame we both have a meeting early tomorrow," she teased.

"Right, Friday." He frowned. "How about I drop you off and come in for a quick nightcap?" He wiggled his eyebrows. "Then, I jet home for a few hours rest."

"I think I'll go home and take a long hot bath. You know," she rubbed her knees, which were still red from their romp on the carpet, "to heal my wounds from the day."

"Yeah, a nice soothing bubble bath sounds good." His smile told her that he was thinking of joining her.

"Alone," she hummed.

"Yeah, I got that. But, if you change your mind . . ."

"You'll be the first one I call," she promised as she twisted her watch.

His eyebrows shot up. "First one?"

She laughed. "Okay, only one."

He nodded, then he raised her hand up to her lips and placed small kisses along her wrist.

When he drove her back to her place, she was having a hard time telling herself not to invite him in. But she needed a little "Amy time" before the busy day she had ahead of her tomorrow. She needed time to think about where their relationship was going. Not to mention their past and what it meant.

He walked her to her door and kissed her as they stood on her front step. When she felt her knees start to shake, he released her and backed away slowly.

"You're making it hard for me to say goodnight," he admitted.

"I am?" She took a few deep breaths so she could think more clearly.

He smiled back at her and she noticed a slight dimple beside his mouth. Why hadn't she ever taken the time to notice that about him?

"See you tomorrow," he whispered, then turned and got back into his car and drove off.

After letting Daisy do her business, she started a bubble bath, and when she had just sunk into the water, her cell phone rang. She couldn't stop the smile from coming to her lips when she saw the name on her screen. Her insides actually heated up even more.

"Are you all settled in the tub yet?" Logan purred.

"Yeah, just got in," she said softly.

She heard him make a noise. "Sorry?" She blinked a few times.

"Sorry, just climbing into mine. It's a great deal smaller than yours." She could hear him moving around and imagined him trying to climb into the small tub she knew he had in his apartment bathroom.

"Since I couldn't join you physically, I thought I'd be there another way."

"I think you're defeating the purpose."

"Oh?" She heard water splash around. "Sorry, banged my knee on the spout. What was that you said?"

She leaned back until most of her body was submerged. "Nothing."

"So," he said after a pause, "what are you wearing?"

She laughed as she rubbed a washcloth over her skin. "I imagine about the same as you are."

"Yeah, but I want to hear you describe it."

She sat up a little. "Are you asking me to have phone sex with you?"

She heard him chuckle. "If you don't want to . . ."

She thought about it, about mentally having his mind roam over every inch of her. "Okay, but you first." She leaned back into the water and continued to circle the cloth around her body as she listened to him describe what he wanted to do to her.

"I want to hear what you're doing right now." She quivered. "Are you touching yourself?"

He was quiet for a moment. "Are you?"

"Yes." It came out as a whisper.

"Where?"

"No, tell me what you're doing first," she teased.

"It doesn't sound as sexy as what you're doing."

"To you maybe. Tell me," she pleaded lightly.

She heard him sigh. "I'm touching myself, thinking about you."

"Where? How?" She settled farther down into the water.

He groaned. "You're killing me."

"Do you want to know what you're doing to me?" She closed her eyes and let her fingers run over her body. The washcloth had disappeared somewhere in the water. "I'm wishing it was your hands on me, running up and down my wet body." She heard him moan softly. "That it was your fingers spreading me, gliding over me."

When he groaned this time, she couldn't stop herself from imagining him touching himself. "Are you stroking yourself?"

She heard him fumble with the phone and tried not to chuckle. "Are you thinking about my mouth on you?" she whispered. "Instead of your hands?"

"Hell yeah." He gasped. "Touch yourself. I want to hear you moan when your fingers slide inside."

She did as he asked and couldn't stop the sound from escaping her lips.

"Yeah, just like that. Imagine my mouth on you, my tongue inside you." Her hips jolted, causing water to splash dangerously close to the edge of her tub. "Pumping in and out." She heard his voice tremble a little. "In and out."

"Come with me," she urged. "Please, Logan."

"I'm right there with you," he said as she shouted his name.

CHAPTER
FOURTEEN

Friday morning meetings always seemed to drag, especially when there wasn't anything really exciting to report. Amy sat in the big meeting room, with over a dozen other employees, and tried not to fall asleep as she listened to Nathan, the account manager, drone on about how to properly fill out time sheets.

Every now and then, she would glance at Logan, but her face would heat when their eyes met. Then she would spend the next few minutes trying to slow her rapid heartbeat back down.

By the end of the meeting, she was all too aware of his eyes on her. The big conference room seemed overly stuffy. Especially with Logan watching her so intently. She knew she had a full day of meetings ahead of her and didn't think she'd be able to maintain any sort of professional attitude if he went with her on any showings.

She watched as his uncle approached him after the meeting and pulled him quickly out the doorway. She was grateful that all her listings were scheduled in the mountains for that day. She could use the twenty-minute drive up the hills to calm herself down.

Less than thirty minutes later, she was climbing into her Jeep and heading out of the parking lot. She hadn't seen Logan since the meeting. She supposed his uncle had kept him busy, since she knew he'd started taking clients of his own now.

The drive up the mountain was peaceful enough and being alone in her car made her feel more centered. She'd never been a fly-by-the-seat-of-her-pants type of person, not like Kristen was at any rate.

Amy had always enjoyed planning out every move she made, every adventure. So when Logan came along, Kristen and her plans to pay him back had seemed the best recourse. Now, however, that list was out. Period.

She remembered what he'd told her that night as they sat along the river. How he'd felt about her all those years ago, not to mention how he'd acted since she'd first seen him walk into the conference room almost a month ago.

Things were moving along with their relationship so fast. Of course, when she'd confessed everything to her best friend, Kristen had done nothing but smile and encourage her to enjoy herself. Amy thought it had more to do with Kristen's own state of mind than anything. After all, why wouldn't you want your best friend to be as happy as you are?

She sighed and took the turn off the highway that led up to her first listing. She was meeting the Lufts and showing them a house that was better suited for a new family. She was thankful that Logan's email had actually encouraged them to take a look at several different houses.

The first one was a little out of their price range. She had mentioned to them that she could possibly talk the seller down. Especially since the house had been on the market for almost six months.

When she drove up, the young couple was already walking around the house. She couldn't help but smile when she saw them holding hands and laughing together.

"Morning," she called out and waved. She could tell by the looks on their faces that they were already in love with the house.

The meeting went quite well and she was sure that this time they would be making an offer. As she drove away, she assured them that if this house wasn't everything they'd dreamed of, she had even more homes to show them.

It was just after lunchtime, and she hadn't had an opportunity yet to grab anything to eat. She'd snacked on a bag of granola she'd shoved into her purse on the way out that morning, but still, her stomach was growling loudly as she drove up to her next appointment.

Noticing there weren't any cars in the driveway yet, she leaned her head back for just a moment. Her phone rang. It was the Lufts with an offer on the last house. She'd had two new offers that day alone. It had taken the Lufts less than fifteen minutes before they agreed to make an offer on the new place. The second offer had come from a single woman for a townhouse in downtown Genesee.

Amy had really liked the townhouse and could have imagined herself living there as well. There was a little more room than she had now, not to mention a large fenced-in yard for the dogs. She started daydreaming about Daisy and her puppies running around a yard while Logan and she cooked out on a large deck.

She was just dreaming up a few kids to run through the yard when she jumped at a knock on her window. A middle-aged man stood outside her car, smiling at her.

"Sorry, looked like you were deep in thought," he said through the glass.

She tried to get her heart to settle before opening the door.

"I'm sorry, I guess it's been a long day." She held out her hand for his. "I'm Amy . . ."

"Yes, I know," he interrupted. "Ray." He held his hand out and she took it. "So, let's have a look at the place." He glanced at the building.

"Yes, if you'll give me a moment." She turned back to her car to get her bag and phone and quickly punched a text to the office.

Then she frowned when her phone came back as no signal. Glancing over her shoulder, she felt like kicking something. This had happened to her enough times in the mountains, she knew better than to panic. After all, she was carrying. Hoisting her bag closer to her, she walked with the man to the front door and waited until he went in. The place wasn't empty, like the rest of her showings, but she knew that the owners were in Florida for three months.

The house was pretty far up in the hills. Far enough that no other homes were in sight. As she showed the man the cabin, she kept her distance and watched him closely. He looked pretty harmless, but then again, she knew the same could be said about many psychopaths.

◆ ◆ ◆

Logan was having one of those days he'd rather forget. Not only had his uncle pulled him into yet another boring meeting, but then he had asked him to help him with an open house he was hosting the following day.

He'd done plenty of open houses during his time with CCR, so he knew the drill. But still his uncle saw fit to walk him through everything. They spent two hours creating fliers, which wouldn't have taken so long had his uncle not accidentally hit delete on the first draft. Then on his way back to Amy's office, Logan'd been asked to help carry signs down to another Realtor's car.

By the time he finally made it back to his and Amy's office, he was dying for some food and hoped she'd want to take a break with him. When he saw that her office was empty yet again, he made his way to Ana's desk to see where Amy was.

"Hey." He stopped just in front of the woman's desk.

Ana glanced up. "She's in Genesee," she chimed in just as her phone rang. Then she held up a finger to have him wait as she answered the call.

"Rocky Mountain Realty, this is Ana."

He watched as Ana listened to the caller, then she frowned up at him.

"No, I'm so sorry she wasn't there to meet you." She listened again and he felt his heart skip a beat. "Yes, of course. I'm sure tomorrow morning will work fine for her." Another pause. "Yes, of course I'll relay the message."

When Ana hung up, he watched her worried look deepen.

"That was the Kimbles. Amy didn't show up for their one o'clock showing."

"Where is she?" He reached for his cell phone and dialed her number, letting it ring as Ana punched away at her computer.

"Her last listing was here." She jotted down an address.

"It's going to voice mail." He looked down at his phone.

Ana picked up her phone and stared at the screen. "I just received this message two minutes ago." She held up her screen so he could read it.

SM showing ok

"I tried to text her, but it bounced back to me. She's probably out of the service area."

"Just in case, I'm heading up there," he said over his shoulder as he rushed toward the stairs.

♦ ♦ ♦

When Amy and Ray walked back out onto the front porch, she turned to him and he said, "I'll take it. That is, if we can close by the end of next month. I already have loan approval and can give you a deposit today." He started to pull out a checkbook from his back pocket.

"I'll contact the sellers and work out all the details. Did you want to make an offer?"

"The asking price seems fair enough," he said as he scribbled on a check. "There, that should cover the deposit. Do you have something for me to sign?" He waited as she took out her standard contract and filled it out.

Ten minutes later she watched his Hummer drive back down the road and smiled. Three offers in one day. It was a new personal record. Maybe her last appointment of the day would turn out to be the fourth one.

She closed up the house and walked back to her Jeep just as the sky opened up and started raining. The weather in the mountains was so unpredictable. Instantly she felt a shiver run down her spine as the cold air hit her.

Jumping into her Jeep, she twisted the key and frowned as nothing happened. Not even a sputter. Trying it again, she pumped the gas a few times. Her Jeep was a few years old, but had never given her problems before.

"No, no," she begged. "Don't do this to me now." She tapped the steering wheel a few times. "Please baby." She tried it again. Nothing. Not even that clinking sound you get when your battery is dead.

Picking up her phone, she felt like screaming when the screen told her she didn't have a signal.

"No!" she moaned. "This cannot be happening!" She rested her head on the wheel as a loud crash of thunder sounded just above her head.

She didn't even want to jump out of her car and race back into the house, since the rain was flooding the muddy driveway. So she sat there until the rain finally let up, which happened to be almost forty minutes later.

Finally, when the skies had cleared, she ventured out. Immediately her shoes sank in the mud. She was thankful that she hadn't chosen to wear heels at least. She'd shown enough houses in the mountains to know better than to wear anything too dressy.

Just as she was opening the front door, she heard a car struggling to make its way up the muddy drive. Turning, she waved when she saw the police SUV. Instantly she knew Ana had called it in when she hadn't shown up for her next appointment.

"Afternoon," the young officer said as he stepped out of his truck. "Are you Amy Walker?" She nodded and stepped off the front porch. "We got a call from your office."

"Yes, thank you. My car doesn't seem to want to start."

She started walking toward him. Then they both turned when they heard another car approaching.

She frowned when she noticed it was Logan's new SUV spitting up mud as he barreled down the driveway.

"Are you okay?" He jumped out of his car and rushed toward her.

"Yes." She took a step back so the mud he was throwing up as he ran to her didn't splatter all over her slacks. "The Jeep won't start." She watched relief wash over him.

"I was just about to look at it," the officer broke in as he walked toward her Jeep.

"I've got it. Thanks," Logan said as his arm went over her shoulders, pulling her close to him.

The officer glanced her way, then between her and Logan. "Will you be okay, miss?"

"Yes, thank you. I'm sorry you made the trek all the way up here." She reached out and shook his hand.

"No problem at all. Sure is a nice place up here." He glanced once more at Logan and walked back to his SUV.

"You scared him off," she joked as they watched the officer disappear down the road. Then she was being pulled into his arms and kissed thoroughly.

"You scared me," he hummed against her neck as he buried his face in her hair.

"I'm sorry." She didn't really understand what he meant.

"Ana got your message that you were up here with a single male client, then we didn't hear from you . . ."

She was beginning to understand. "Logan." She leaned back and placed her hands on either side of his face. "I'm sorry. I didn't mean to scare anyone. My Jeep has never acted up before, then it was pouring down rain and I didn't want to get hit by lightning." She glanced over at the Jeep, then turned back to him. "Besides, I was on a roll. Three offers today. I was hoping for my fourth."

"Three? I guess we'll have to go out and celebrate." She could see that he was relaxing more.

He hugged her one more time. "Come on, I'll take a look under the hood."

She rushed to keep in step with him. "Do you know anything about cars?"

"Every man knows about cars." He turned to her. "Or they should, anyway." He flipped open her Jeep hood and looked in. "Guess we know why it's not starting." He held up the electric wires that she knew should have been attached to the battery. "Looks like they bounced loose on the drive up." He glanced over to the muddy driveway and she remembered hitting a particularly deep rut on the way up. "Try it now," he said after attaching the cables again.

She walked over and jumped back into the seat, and this time when she turned the key, her Jeep instantly sprang to life.

She smiled up at him as he shut and secured her hood. "I'll want to tighten the nuts down when I have some tools. I'll follow you back."

She leaned out her open window. "I still owe you drinks." She watched his eyes light up. "For losing at pool."

"Yes, you do."

"How about we hit Main Street Pub and Grill?" She glanced down at his muddy feet, then her own. "After we change."

"It's a date. I'll swing by and pick you up." He tapped her hood. "Just in case."

Logan was so different from the boy who had bullied her. Gone was the selfish kid who took and destroyed.

He leaned in her window and kissed her until she felt her body melt.

CHAPTER
FIFTEEN

Main Street Pub and Grill was crowded. Logan felt wonderful walk-ing into the pub holding Amy's hand. Then she started tugging on him until they stopped in front of the table with her friends Kristen Collins and Aiden Scott, head of Urban Development. He'd met Aiden on sev-eral occasions when he'd worked for CCR.

"Hey." Amy smiled down at the couple, who looked like they'd been about to order food. When Kristen looked up, the two friends giggled and hugged each other like they hadn't seen each other in years instead of days.

"Aiden." He held out his hand. "Logan Miller."

Aiden nodded. "We've met. I think you were working with Tiffany?"

Logan groaned and rolled his eyes. "Right, I'm at Rocky Mountain Realty now." He sat when Aiden motioned for them to join them. "Actually, my uncle owns RMR."

"I remember Kristen telling me you'd moved back to Golden."

He glanced at the two friends with their heads bent together. He leaned closer to Aiden. "Do you think they planned this?"

"I was wondering why she wanted to have dinner in Golden tonight. We usually come up here to see her folks once a month, but their visit was last weekend."

They chuckled as the waitress walked up to the table.

"Beer and the Reuben?" Logan asked Amy, who nodded in reply, then continued to talk with Kristen.

Once their drinks were delivered, everyone started talking about Amy's ordeal. He was pleased when Kristen showed just as much concern as he had about the entire situation.

"I can't stand that you're out of range half the time." Kristen met Logan's eyes briefly. "Especially after what happened a few years back."

He watched Amy's eyes roll. "We're very careful at RMR. Besides, I think every Realtor has changed their tactics since then."

"Nothing will stop a psycho from killing."

"We're not even safe in a movie theater, or for that matter, sitting in a pub on a Friday night." Amy leaned forward and patted her friend's hand. "I'm careful, you know me." Kristen reached over and hugged her friend. "Besides, aren't you the one who almost died in an elevator?" Amy winked at Aiden, then started laughing.

An hour later, Logan had to admit that he was happy they'd run into the other couple. It was quite funny to see how different Kristen and Amy were. Even more, the differences between Aiden and Kristen were almost shocking. Especially seeing how well they made it work.

It was actually Aiden and Amy who had a lot in common, at least of what Logan could see. They both were super organized and very meticulous about the way they ate. He tried to hold back a chuckle as the two of them actually helped clear the table by stacking their plates for the waitress once all the food was gone.

He'd been at Amy's house several times now. Not a thing was out of place, just like her. There wasn't a hair on her head that wasn't where it should be. Her clothes looked like they had all been neatly pressed and laundered before she even set foot outside.

He looked at her next to him, remembering the times when her hair was tangled in his hands. When her clothes were crinkled from being thrown on the floor. How she looked panting underneath him.

He took her hand in his. She leaned closer to him and he wrapped his arm around her shoulders.

"So, are you two going to the DMRA party together?" Kristen asked, resting her chin on her hands as she looked at them.

"DMRA?" he questioned.

She chuckled. "Denver Metro Realtor Association party, it's in a month."

He remembered it now. He'd actually gone to the party once, with Bella. He glanced over at Amy and saw excitement in her eyes.

"I'd planned on it," he fibbed and was quickly rewarded with her smile.

"If you like parties, what about . . ."

"Don't even think about it. Not yet." Amy glared at Kristen as she twisted her watch vigorously. He could see she was nervous about what her friend was trying to say.

"Why not?" Kristen's smile spread slowly on her face. "You know, it's only four months away. Besides, I just bet he'd like to go."

"To what?" He glanced between the two friends.

"Our wedding," Aiden piped in.

He looked at Amy and felt a little uneasy as thoughts of his parents' marriage flew through his mind. He didn't know one couple who had made marriage work, nor did he think it was possible at this point.

"See, now you've scared him." Amy squeezed his hand as he tried to deny it.

Kristen and Amy laughed. "That is the same face you made when you tried to hide the fact that you'd TP'd Mr. Ragan's car in grade school. It was the reason you had a month's detention," Kristen joked.

He laughed and then smiled at Kristen. "Tell you what, if you save a dance for me, I'll be there."

"Then it's a date," Kristen jumped in.

◆ ◆ ◆

When Logan pulled his car to a stop in front of her place, Amy turned to him. "I should have warned you about inviting them," she said.

"It turned out okay." Still, he wished she would have opened up to him more and told him why she'd felt the need to invite them.

She glanced over at him. "Call it one of my knee-jerk impulses."

He brushed a hand down her hair. "Why?"

She blinked and tilted her head. "Why what?"

"Why did you have that impulse? Why invite them tonight?"

She leaned back in the seat. "I've been feeling a little overwhelmed."

"About us?" he interjected.

"We do have quite a history."

He chuckled. "Fair enough. But, I thought things were going well."

She didn't want to tell him why she'd freaked out. The truth was, she didn't even know. She'd felt the need to be alone the other night, but when he'd called, she'd found herself falling into his web. And, more importantly, she'd enjoyed it.

There wasn't a part of her life that she hadn't planned out completely. Becoming a partner at RMR was and should be her number one priority. Fraternizing with the competition wasn't going to get her closer to her goal.

"I haven't had any long-term relationships," she blurted out. "Not like you." She waited.

"Okay." His smile was reassuring.

"The longest relationship I've had lasted two weeks." Closing her eyes, she rested her head back on the headrest. Then, his fingers tangled in her hair, gently pulling her face until she was looking at him.

"Because of knee-jerk impulses?"

"I've seen relationships go south. I guess it's my way of avoidance." That and her desperate need to control everything. Ever since the night her mother had thrown all her belongings into boxes, she'd felt a deep urge to keep everything in its place.

He started moving his hand to her neck. "I'm not going anywhere," he said right before his mouth touched hers softly.

When he broke the kiss, she relaxed. "How about coming inside for a nightcap?"

His smile was quick, then he rested his forehead on hers. "I'll take a rain check. I've got an early morning meeting."

Her eyebrows arched in question.

"I'm showing the listing you missed today. Early," he added.

"I could . . ."

His finger went over her lips as he shook his head. "Not until I replace your battery cables and make sure you won't get stranded again."

She thought about getting stuck again, then nodded slowly. "Okay, I'll give you this one."

"Besides, Kristen only mentioned it a dozen times that you two are dress shopping tomorrow."

She giggled. "Yes, so she did."

"Have fun." He leaned over and kissed her again.

After letting Daisy out, she had a hard time getting to sleep that night. Maybe it was the loneliness she was feeling. For the first time, she was missing one man in particular.

The conversation from the evening kept playing over in her head. She had been nervous when Kristen had mentioned the wedding to Logan. After all, she knew by the way he'd talked about his parents' marriage that he didn't think too highly of the institution. Come to think of it, neither did she. But she was a woman and part of her kept dreaming that someday she'd find the perfect man and they would live happily ever after. But was it Logan?

She was thankful when Daisy jumped up on the bed with her and snuggled down. She'd moved the bed of dogs into her room for the night.

Logan had taken them to the vet the other day. It was the first time she'd trusted a man with a key to her place, which he'd promptly returned after letting her know that Daisy was current with her shots and the puppies had been given a clean bill of health. They would need their puppy shots when they were a little older. When she'd gotten home that night, she couldn't help but smile at all the extras he'd bought for the small family.

Daisy had a new dog bed, toys, collar, and a matching leash. Even though the dog never left her side when she took her on short walks, she knew it was city ordinance and had used it ever since. He'd also purchased a larger whelping box for the puppies to be in and doggy pee pads for the nursery. Amy had laughed when she noticed that each puppy had her very own individually colored collar that they could easily grow into.

Finally, she settled down with Daisy snuggled next to her.

The next morning, she woke when her phone chimed. Reaching over, she glanced at the screen and read the text message, then jumped out of bed. She pulled on a bathrobe as she rushed to her front door.

"Morning." Logan smiled back at her as he handed her a cup of coffee and held up a box. "Donuts?"

She stood back when Daisy ran out the door to do her business.

"How are they doing?" He looked back toward her guest room.

"Wonderful. I moved them in with me," she said, then took a sip of her coffee. It was just the way she liked it and she moaned when the sweetness started to rush through her.

"Oh?" he said.

"I was lonely. Besides, Daisy likes to escape the puppy box and jumps up on the bed with me every now and then," she added, reaching down to twirl her bracelet as she looked up at him.

He walked in and set the box of donuts down. "I figured you'd want some extra sugar to get you going. Especially if you're going to spend the day trying on bridesmaid dresses." She thought she saw him cringe but wasn't sure. Most men hated thinking about weddings, or spending time dress shopping. She could tell Logan was no different.

"Of course, after eating a few of those," she glanced down at the chocolate-covered goodness and felt her stomach growl, "I'll have to try on dresses that are two sizes bigger."

He took her by the shoulders and smiled at her. "You'd have to eat a truckload. I know it's early, but I wanted to stop by before I head into the mountains."

"I could still . . ."

He stopped her by wrapping his arms around her. "Don't even think about it. Besides, I have another showing before I'm supposed to help my uncle with an open house."

She settled into his arms feeling wonderful. He smelled sexy, causing her to wish they had the entire day to themselves.

"Now, let's eat. I'm starved," he suggested.

"You're always hungry," she joked.

His fingers tightened on her hips. "At least when I'm around you."

She felt her pulse kick as his fingers brushed through her hair. Only then did she realize that she had just rushed to the door without even brushing her hair or teeth.

"Have I told you how sexy you look in the morning?" He leaned closer to her and ran his lips across hers.

She shook her head.

"Hmmm, sweet too." His mouth played over hers until they heard the puppies crying and watched Daisy come back in through the open front door.

♦　♦　♦

When Logan left, she rushed around the house getting ready for her day with Kristen. When she was almost ready, Kristen surprised her by texting that she was on her way to pick her up.

What do you mean? Pick me up?

Aiden hired us a car for the day. Come outside.

After picking up her bag, she locked her door and walked out. She was totally shocked to see a long white limo pull into her parking lot.

"Aiden did this?" she asked as Kristen jumped out from the back door before the driver could walk around and open it for her.

"Yup, it's all ours for the day." Kristen giggled and hugged her. "Have you had breakfast?"

"I've had enough sugar to fill that limo," she said as she climbed in the back. Amber, Aiden's half sister, was already sitting on the long seat. Ashley, Aiden's youngest sister, was spending the summer abroad, but would be home in time for the wedding in mid-November.

Their first stop was at a bagel shop to get Kristen a sandwich and coffee. The second was to pick up Reagan, another bridesmaid, then Stephany and lastly Carolyn.

Then the five women hit the first bridal shop on a long list Amy had printed out for Kristen. Amy was taking her role as maid of honor very seriously.

By the fourth shop, they had found the bridesmaids' dresses. They were long, flowing, spaghetti-strap dresses in different colors, since Kristen couldn't narrow her wedding colors down to just one shade. Amy chose the pink for herself, and Amber chose a softer blue. Then Stephany looked stunning in burgundy, and Carolyn chose the purple, while Reagan chose a light yellow.

After the shop had fitted everyone for their dresses, they headed out to the next shop with only one goal. To find the perfect wedding dress.

Kristen was such a free-spirited person, no one dress suited her best. At least that's what Amy thought, until just after they had stopped off at Olive Garden for lunch.

The next shop was nestled in historic Cherry Hills. Amy spotted the dress the moment they walked in.

The narrow straps that held up the soft white silk would look perfect on Kristen. The skirt of the dress was covered with an older-looking lace and flowed all the way to the floor then made a longer train.

When Kristen tried it on, everyone else agreed that this was the dress. They looked around the store for a veil, but then Amy got an idea.

"What do you think about us making your veil?" She'd watched the process on a show a few months back and had wanted to try it ever since. Besides, it had looked like fun and she loved doing crafts with Kristen.

"What?" Kristen looked confused.

"Sure, it's not like we have to sew anything. I mean, what I was imagining is something simple." She walked over to the counter and asked the clerk for a pencil and paper. Then sketched out what she had envisioned. "Something like this."

She turned the paper around and showed the other ladies.

"Oh, it's perfect." Kristen exclaimed. "But, how . . ."

"We can sell you the material," the clerk who'd been helping them said. "Here." They all stood back as she began digging through boxes. "Everything you'll need except a hot glue gun and needle and thread."

"This is going to be so much fun," Carolyn said, jumping up and down.

So, the next stop was to Amy's house again, since they didn't want to go back to Kristen and Aiden's apartment in case he happened to show up.

Everyone cooed over the puppies for a while before they opened a couple bottles of wine and dug into their new project.

"We've ordered our announcements," Kristen said as she pulled out an envelope from her bag. For the next few minutes, everyone enjoyed passing the card around. "We're going to include this picture." She handed over a picture that Amy had taken of the pair with her cell phone when they had gone on a hiking trip near Red Rocks.

"It's perfect," she said, smiling at her friend.

Spending the entire day thinking about and planning her friend's wedding made it hard to keep her mind off her own future wedding. Which only made her think of Logan.

She was growing more sure of their relationship. He was going out of his way to show her how much he cared for her, which was making her feel even closer to him than before.

By the time the third bottle of wine was done, they had put together the most beautiful veil she'd ever seen. It was a simple ring that would fit over Kristen's curly hair, covered in dainty flowers and baby's breath. The veil part hung in the back, down past her shoulders and had a floral mesh design all around the edges. Part of the veil would swing over and cover Kristen's face, since she wanted Aiden to lift it in the ceremony. They had attached a larger silk flower to one side of the ring, which matched the design on the shoulder of her wedding dress perfectly.

"Wow, we should go into business making these," Amber joked as she drank another sip of her water. She was a singer and had a performance later that evening, and she wanted to be fresh and alert.

"Why not?" Kristen smiled. "Or better yet, host parties for brides and let them make their own." Everyone giggled.

Just then, there was a knock on the door. When Amy walked over, she couldn't hide the smile as she peeked and saw who was standing outside.

When she opened the door, Logan's eyes traveled around the messy crowded room. "Uh." She watched him take a step backward.

"Oh, no you don't." She grabbed him by the shirt and pulled him to her until her bare feet touched the tips of his shoes. "Everyone this is Logan, Logan . . . everyone." She giggled, then turned back to him and saw him smiling down at her.

"Looks like I missed the party," he said to the room.

"We were just finishing up." Kristen said. "Amy, I'm going to hang this in your guest-room closet. I can't take it back to my place and have Aiden finding it." Her friend carried her veil into the other room.

"Yes, I need to get back. I've got a performance in a few hours." Amber glanced at her watch.

"We should be going too." The other ladies looked among themselves with smiles on their faces.

CHAPTER
SIXTEEN

Logan hadn't planned on Amy's house being crowded with women or that her place would look like a tornado of lace and silk had blown through it. He was happily surprised to see her slightly drunk and held onto her when she teetered as her friends left.

"Well"—she turned and wrapped her arms around his neck—"now it's just us." She leaned up and placed a kiss on his lips.

He chuckled until the kiss stirred something deep inside. Then he was pulling her closer and wishing she was sober so he could enjoy himself.

When he stepped back, she frowned up at him.

"How about some dinner?" he asked.

"Food is good. I could eat." She swayed, so he took her shoulders and steered her toward the sofa.

"You sit. I'll prepare us something."

"You?" She stopped dead, almost causing him to trip over her. Then she turned around and looked up at him. "Cook?"

"I've been out on my own for a while now. I have learned a thing or two in the kitchen."

She snorted with laughter. "I remember your moves in the kitchen."

He chuckled and pushed on her shoulders until she fell back on the sofa. "Sit."

By the time he was done scrounging around her kitchen, he knew there was no way he was making anything without a quick stop at a store. When he walked back out to her living room, Amy was curled up and fast asleep on the sofa.

Being extra quiet, he took her house keys and locked up behind him.

When he returned half an hour later with two large bags of groceries, she was still fast asleep with Daisy curled up at her feet.

He tried to be as quiet as he could as he cooked garlic-roasted salmon on a bed of seasoned Brussels sprouts. One of his favorite and better meals.

By the time he'd set her table and lit her candles, he heard her moving around in the other room. When she walked into the dining room, his smile froze a little. She'd changed into a flowing dress and had loosened her hair from the braid she'd worn earlier.

"Hi." He felt his mouth go dry as he looked at her.

"Hi." She walked toward him. "Something smells wonderful." She leaned up and placed a soft kiss on his cheek. His hands went to her hips, holding her close to him as he buried his face in her hair.

"Mmm, yes, something *does* smell wonderful."

When they finally sat down to eat, he was having an even harder time keeping his eyes off her. He watched every small move she made, focusing on her lips especially.

When their plates were empty, they moved into her living room, which he noticed she'd taken the time to clean while he'd been cooking.

"How about some music?" she asked as she walked over to her stereo and punched a button. Instead of soft music flowing out, Bruce Springsteen's "Born in the U.S.A." pumped out loudly.

She laughed and quickly turned the music down. "Sorry, I was listening to this while I was cleaning the house yesterday." She flipped on her CD player and soft music played instead.

"I like both." He took her hips and moved with her. "Just as long as you're my dance partner." He leaned down and kissed her until he felt her shiver.

◆ ◆ ◆

Amy lay in Logan's arms and stared up at the ceiling. The hour nap she'd taken earlier left her wide awake while he slept silently next to her. It felt wonderful to be in his arms, so close to his naked body. Her ear was pressed up against his chest and she could hear his steady heartbeat. Daisy had jumped up on the bed shortly after Logan had pulled the covers over their cooling bodies.

Images of the day flashed in her mind as she thought about her friend's happiness and her own. Kristen was marrying the man of her dreams and she couldn't be happier for both of them.

Which of course, got her thinking about the man of her dreams. Growing up, she'd had a plan. She probably still had the list somewhere of the traits she thought made up her perfect husband.

She moved to glance up at Logan and realized he probably didn't have one thing in common with the man on her list. But maybe that's why this was working so well between them? Maybe she was being too picky? Kristen was always telling her she was. She felt the need to be guarded—after all, Amy had grown up watching Kristen fall in love with every blond-haired boy with blue eyes. Then, she'd been there after each of those relationships had shattered to pick her friend up. Then there was the way her parents' marriage had ended. Who could blame her for being cautious?

Settling her head back on his shoulder, she nestled in when his arm automatically came up around her. Shutting down her mind for the night, she decided to let fate take its course.

◆　◆　◆

By the end of the following weeks, she was seriously questioning why she had doubted anything about their relationship in the first place. Especially since everything was going so well.

So, why then was she finding herself more and more on edge? Because she knew, just knew, something was about to blow up. After all, it always had. Every relationship she'd ever had, no matter how short it'd been, had ended the same way. Still, he was doing so much right, which only made her wonder further when it would all end.

Logan had started staying with her most nights. Although, anytime she felt like she needed her space, he would go back to his place and leave her to herself, which hadn't been too often.

Even at work he'd gone out of his way for her. He'd shown up and helped her for an open house she'd had one weekend. She had always hated sitting in a house alone, waiting for people to walk in. Since he'd been there, the time had flown.

Toward the end of August, Kristen had taken her dress shopping and she'd picked out a beautiful, short and sassy, teal party dress for the DMRA party, which was quickly approaching. Kristen had told her that Aiden had been invited by one of his clients and so she'd picked out a dress for herself. Her dress, however, was a little more off the shelf. She'd actually picked out a bright red wrap that had a hint of the Orient. When Kristen had walked out of the dressing room wearing it, Amy knew that it was the perfect dress for her friend.

Gary had not mentioned any of his plans for the agency to either Logan or her. Or at least Logan wasn't talking about it if his uncle had discussed it with him. It wasn't as if she'd asked Gary if Logan was being prepped for partnership in the agency. She'd been a little too nervous to walk in and ask him. She had tried to work up the courage several times, but so far hadn't been able to open her mouth. As far as she could tell, his uncle had just brought him on board to handle the extra load they'd been getting the last year. But in reality, maybe she was scared of the answer at this point.

Actually, she'd overheard Gary mentioning leasing part of the third floor in their building next year since they were hiring on a few other people. Which, in her mind, assured her that he'd need at least one partner to handle the increased business.

On Saturday, the day before the big party, her nerves were so wired, she'd even taken it out on Kristen, who had just called to see if she could snap a picture of her veil and send it to her. Feeling bad that she'd been short with her best friend, she took a few extra minutes and sent Kristen half a dozen shots.

She was so tense, Logan had even abandoned ship and was spending the night at his own place. It wasn't as if she'd been mean to him, maybe just a little distant. Which he'd quickly picked up on and made some excuse that he'd had to go to his uncle's and help him clean out his garage.

She knew that her mood had more to do with how everything was progressing. Her relationship with Logan had never been better, which scared her even more. She'd always lived life waiting for the other shoe to drop. Ever since the night her mother had woken her up packing her things and threatening to move. She had learned then that it was better to be guarded than trusting. Which was probably why all of her past relationships had ended so poorly. All except her friendship with Kristen.

She was just getting around to making herself some dinner, when her doorbell rang. Daisy had taken to barking after hearing the sound and started telling her loudly that someone was at the door.

"Yes, I heard it." She rolled her eyes at the small dog as she looked out the security hole before opening the door slowly.

"Flowers for Amy Walker." A delivery woman stood outside her doorway.

She nodded, not sure what to say. No one had ever sent her flowers before. The woman handed her the large bouquet before telling her to have a good evening.

The first thing Amy did when the door was shut was to bury her face in the sweet-smelling flowers. The second thing was to rip open the card that was attached to the silver vase.

For no reason other than that I'm thinking of you. —Logan

The vise around her heart loosened a little as she set the flowers down on her coffee table. She cried as she looked at them.

When her pity party was over, she searched for her cell phone and texted him.

Thanks for the flowers. They're lovely.

You're welcome. I miss you.

She sat and tucked her feet up underneath her on her oversized chair and glanced out the window. She was being ridiculous. Here she was waiting around for something bad to happen and she was the one causing the rift between them.

Maybe when you're done helping your uncle, you can come back here?

Are you sure?

Ever the safe one, she thought.

Yeah, I miss you too.

Less than five minutes later, she heard a knock on the door, and when she opened it, Logan was leaning against her doorjamb with another handful of flowers.

"I'm not trying to bribe you or anything," he said.

"You could have fooled me." She reached for the flowers, only to have him pull them away.

"Oh, no. These ones come with a price." He tapped his lips with his finger. She went up on her toes and placed a slow kiss on his lips.

After he handed her the bouquet, he took his turn and leaned down to kiss her softly. "Your change."

She bunched her fist in his shirt and pulled him through her doorway. Then setting the flowers on the table, she shoved him up against the closed door and kissed him hard.

Fast. She needed and wanted him as quickly as possible. Her fingers shook as she pushed his clothes off him. Shoving and even, at one point, ripping his shirt over his head.

He smelled of musk and sweat, a scent that intoxicated her as she ran her mouth over his chest. He'd fisted his hands in her hair, but when she leaned back to pull his pants off, he quickly started tugging at her clothes.

He backed her up to the sofa and they fell onto the cushions together, naked. She didn't have time to think or breathe before he was pulling her legs up and plunging into her. Her nails dug into his hips, pushing and pulling to make him go faster.

"More." He growled next to her neck. "I'll have it all," he murmured as his eyes met hers. She was mesmerized at how blue they were, how much she saw in the crystal pools. She held on while he took everything she willingly gave him.

CHAPTER
SEVENTEEN

There was little time for them to talk the next morning before the party. She'd rushed over to pick Kristen up so they could go shoe shopping, since Amy didn't have a pair that went with her dress. She'd thought she'd had a teal pair of heels when she'd bought the dress, but couldn't find them anywhere.

It was a sign, at least in her mind, that she was losing her focus. That was one of the reasons she'd flipped out the day before. She loved control and order. Lived for it actually. She didn't like it when things weren't orderly. So, in general, when she noticed in life that she'd started forgetting things, or misplacing items, she would freeze up and hit reverse as quickly as she could. Memories would surface of living in boxes while her parents decided what they wanted to do. She hated when she felt this way.

Thank goodness for Logan and those flowers. Without them, she would have probably freaked out. She'd stared at them for so long that her mind had finally settled down and relaxed.

After an uneventful ride, she parked outside Kristen and Aiden's building in downtown Denver to wait for her friend to come rushing out.

"Hey, sorry I'm late," Kristen said, jumping into her Jeep.

"You're not." She smiled over at her. "I'm late."

Kristen's looked at her in utter disbelief.

"What?" Amy frowned. "I can be late every now and then."

Kristen shook her head slowly. "Who are you?" she joked.

Amy laughed. "It's Logan's fault. He bought me flowers."

"As in . . ."

"Delivered. Then he showed up with even more."

Kristen giggled as Amy pulled onto the street. "You've got it bad. So, do you think he's the one?"

Amy almost swerved as she quickly glanced over at her friend. "No!"

"Well," Kristen pouted. "Why not? After all, Aiden isn't exactly who I pictured falling for when we were kids either." She looked out her window, daydreaming. "But, I wouldn't want to be marrying any other man."

"I know, it's just . . ." She didn't know what to say. Actually, she was completely speechless. She'd done nothing but think about their relationship for the last few days. One thing was clear after last night, she knew she wanted to enjoy him for as long as she could. Shaking, she turned and parked in the mall lot. When she turned off her car, she looked at her friend. "Logan is . . . Our relationship is . . ."

"Ha!" Kristen pointed her finger at her. "When you can't define it, it is beyond definition."

"That doesn't make any sense."

Kristen shrugged. "It will when you least expect it." Her friend got out of the Jeep. "Now, let's go find you some shoes and get pedicures." Kristen linked her arm through Amy's as they started walking toward the mall entrance.

◆ ◆ ◆

Logan glanced at himself one last time in Amy's guest bathroom mirror. He didn't mind wearing a tux, especially since a few years back he'd paid to have his very own made. It fit like a glove, or fit like he'd imagined James Bond's tux fit.

He'd slicked his hair back and twisted his head one way, then the other to make sure his barber had evened out his sides. Nothing was out of place.

When Amy had told him that she'd never had flowers delivered, he'd arranged for even more of them to be delivered. They would arrive any minute. He glanced at his watch. They had less than an hour before they were to be in downtown Denver.

Walking out of the bathroom, he was just about to head toward the front door, when the doorbell chimed. Daisy darted from Amy's room barking madly.

"Yes, Daisy, we all heard the door . . ." His words fell away when he spotted Amy standing in her doorway. The light teal dress clung to her curves. The skirt was fluffed and short, showing off the best pair of legs he'd ever had the pleasure of seeing. Her open-toe heels were the same color as her dress, as were her earrings and necklace. There was even a small bracelet around her left wrist that sparkled with teal.

Her long hair was piled on top of her head as small ringlets hung around her face and down her back.

"Well, are you going to answer it?" she asked as she started walking toward him.

He could only shake his head no.

She chuckled and glided past him to open the door. That's when he noticed that most of the back of the dress was missing. He could see all the way to the curve of her lower back, which only made his tux pants tighter on him.

"Oh!" she exclaimed, causing his eyes to rush to her face as she spun around. "More flowers?"

He smiled and started to wonder if he was going to be stricken mute all night while in her presence.

He'd ordered white flowers this time and watched her bury her face into their softness. He must have moaned, because her eyes moved back up to him.

"Are you okay?" She frowned.

He started to walk toward her, a slow smile forming on his lips. "You look amazing." His fingers gently touched her hips, since he didn't want to mess her up anywhere.

He thought he saw her cheeks blush as she looked up at him. "Thank you. You look very sexy." Her fingers went to his neck as she straightened the already straight tie. "We'd better get going if we plan on being there on time."

He leaned down and brushed a soft kiss on her cheek. He watched her set the flowers down on the kitchen table then walk over to grab a small silver purse from the chair.

"I'm ready," she said.

When they walked into the Four Seasons' lobby, they ran into Kristen and Aiden. The pair looked amazing as they made their way across the floor toward them.

"Evening." He nodded toward Aiden.

"How's it going?" He shook his hand firmly. "So, we're up on the third floor."

He walked shoulder to shoulder with Aiden as the women walked in front of them, whispering.

"Are they always like this?" he asked Aiden right before they stepped into the elevator.

Aiden glanced at the pair, then back at him. "Always," he said with a smile.

When they stepped out of the elevator, it was onto an open terrace with a swimming pool. Since they were there an hour before sunset, the colors of the sky were breathtaking. There were already over a hundred people standing around, drinking, and talking as they signed in.

Logan immediately saw his uncle across the bar with Leah close by his side. The larger woman looked nice in a very long, flowing blue dress. Her hair was arranged softly around her face, making her look younger.

"There's my uncle." He touched Amy's arm and pointed toward the bar.

"Shall we go say hello?" She smiled as the group made their way toward the bar area. Logan ordered drinks for them, then leaned against the bar to listen to his uncle tell one of his crazy stories to another Realtor.

"Look at Gary," Kristen whispered to Amy. "He was born for this." She giggled as Logan's uncle finished the story of how he'd persuaded an elderly couple to remove the close to four hundred gnomes that had inhabited their yard so their house would sell.

"He's always had good stories." Amy turned to Kristen. "Remember our tenth birthday party at your folks' place? He had all the girls convinced that he was Prince Charming." They laughed and Logan felt a pang of longing for a childhood that never happened. As he watched his uncle, he wished more than anything that his mother had chosen to remain close to her brother despite being married to her husband.

"Hey." Amy broke into his thoughts of all the missed fun and family times as a child. "Are you okay?"

He blinked and glanced down at her, then ran a hand over her shoulder. "Yeah, fine." He looked over and saw a few of his old coworkers. "I'm going to go say hello to some people."

"Want me to tag along?" she asked.

He shook his head, not wanting to tell her he needed a moment alone. "I'll be quick." He left his drink at the bar and made his way toward Derrick and John, two of his old colleagues at CCR.

When he approached the two men, he was shocked to see Tiffany standing in front of them. She wore an almost sheer white gown and, in the dying light, the sparkles on her dress caused almost a glow around her. Her long blonde hair was down around her shoulders in soft waves. There were diamonds around her neck and in her ears, no doubt bought by her father, who had always given his only daughter anything she'd ever asked for.

Quickly, he thought about turning back around, but it was too late when she squealed loudly and rushed to hug him.

"There you are," she purred. "I've been looking all over for you." Her fingers dug into his hair, messing it up. "We were just talking about the good old days," she said as she ran a manicured fingernail up his chest, stopping just below his chin.

"Tiff," he said, then he nodded in Derrick and John's direction.

"Tiffany was just telling us how her father has called off her wedding to Marcus," Derrick said, waggling his eyebrows behind her back.

"Oh?" He felt the evening air start to warm.

"Yes, it was mean of Daddy to try and force me into that relationship." She stuck out her full bottom lip in a pout.

His mind instantly raced to another lip he'd kissed that looked much better in that position. Trying to twist his body to see if Amy was still at the bar, he groaned when he noticed her walking their way. That sexy little frown was firmly in place on her lips as she watched Tiffany wrap her body around his.

"Listen, Tiff . . ." he started to say, just before she moved her body even closer to his. Now he felt like they were smashed together, and he was having a difficult time breathing as panic started to set in.

He felt Amy stop beside him.

"I believe you have your body wrapped around my boyfriend." Amy's voice sounded calm as she spoke.

He wasn't given the opportunity to speak before Tiffany chuckled loudly and ran her eyes up and down Amy's dress. "I highly doubt that," she purred as her fingers dug into his hair, trying to pull him down for a kiss.

His entire body tensed as he tried to push the clinging woman away. He thought he heard Amy growl slightly, then knew he was in trouble before even seeing Amy's reaction. He watched the reaction of Derrick and John and took the hint that he needed to duck, quickly.

Not even dislodging himself from Tiffany's hold, he bent at the waist and missed the stream of liquid that would have hit him directly in the back. Spinning around, he watched a very angry Amy storm toward the elevators.

When the high-pitch screaming finally reached his mind, he turned back around to see Tiffany, soaking wet, glaring at Amy's back.

"Who is that bitch?" she screamed and started storming toward Amy.

Logan ran after both women and beat Amy to the elevators. He spun her around. "It's not what it looked like," he started to say, only to be interrupted by a very pissed-off Tiffany.

"I don't know who you think you are, but I'll have you banned from . . ." Logan stepped between them quickly.

"Leave it to me," he growled in Tiffany's direction while he held Amy still so she wouldn't jump into the waiting elevator.

He watched the fight leave Tiffany's eyes, then she poured on the purr again and stepped closer to him until her soaking wet breasts were pushed up against his jacket. "Fine, I'll just head upstairs and change into my backup dress. I'm in room number sixteen oh one." She discreetly put a card in his jacket pocket.

"Listen, Tiff," he started to say again, only to have Amy twist in his arms.

"Hold still," he said, tightening his hold on her.

"This is Amy, I'm with her now," he blurted out quickly, since he knew there wasn't enough time to do it properly.

He watched Tiffany's eyes zero in on Amy, then a slight smile curved on her lips. "Oh." She chuckled. "Really Logan, you could do so much better . . ."

Now he was holding Amy back from scratching Tiffany's eyes out as Tiffany laughed even more.

"Logan, you'd better cage your new bitch." She walked toward the waiting elevators.

He tugged on Amy's hand, but she didn't budge. So he picked her up and carried her toward a private cabana area, securing the doors and locking them in.

"Would you like to tell me what all that was about?" He crossed his arms over his chest, blocking her escape from the door.

Instead of speaking, she crossed her arms over her chest and mimicked his stance. "Would you like to tell me what all that was about?" She finally repeated his question to him.

"That was Tiffany."

"Yes, so I gathered," she interrupted.

He prayed for patience. "Remember, I told you we used to go out." She waited.

"Well, it appears that her father has released her of her obligation to marry . . ."

"Yes, I heard that part. So did everyone else on the terrace."

He leaned his shoulders back against the closed doors.

"I didn't know she was over there. I swear. If I had I never would have . . ."

Her eyes narrowed and he chose that moment to shut his mouth. Instead of speaking, he walked over to her and took her by the hips. "I don't want to be with anyone other than you," he whispered into her hair. He could feel her anger vibrating within her. He pulled back and looked deep into her blue eyes then rested his forehead against hers. "Honest."

He felt her sigh, then her hands went up to his hair. He smiled as she finger combed it back into place. "Okay, but if she comes near you again tonight . . ."

"Trust me, she won't." He leaned down and kissed her until he felt her melt against him. Just the thought of her leaving him had his body shaking.

"Where do we go from here?" she asked when he finally paused for a breath.

He took her hand in his and pulled it up to his lips. "Wherever it is, we'll do it together." He had never spoken truer words than those. No matter what came at him, he knew he wanted her by his side. That thought alone scared him.

When they walked out of the cabana a few minutes later, the entire two hundred guests on the terrace clapped and cheered. He turned in time to see Amy's cheeks turn pink with embarrassment, and he couldn't help himself from twirling her around as they laughed.

CHAPTER
EIGHTEEN

Logan and Amy had made such a hit, they'd been deemed the honorary King and Queen of the party. He was relieved that Tiffany hadn't shown up again the entire night. Amy had been embarrassed for a while after the little show, but he had managed to get her out on the dance floor several times. By the end of the night, she had relaxed and he could tell that she'd enjoyed the evening.

The next day at work, his uncle had bragged that he had another funny story to tell everyone who hadn't shown up for the party. Amy had blushed, but had taken all the teasing in stride.

There was very little time over the rest of the week for Logan to spend with Amy at work. When he finally left the office, he would head over to her place and they would spend their nights together. But some days they were stuck at the office until after dark.

He'd talked with his uncle about hiring on some more staff and had been told he was looking into it. They had all heard the rumor that his uncle was also looking into leasing some space on the floor above and would be turning those into the executive offices. But so far his uncle hadn't said a word to him about it.

He'd taken on a large number of his own listings and had a full schedule of showings just like most of the other Realtors in the agency.

By the next Friday morning, he was completely exhausted. He knew he and Amy had a full day of showings ahead of them. He was sad that they no longer went on showings together; he missed the extra time with her. He knew they couldn't afford to until they hired more employees.

He watched her pull out of the parking lot and felt his heart skip a beat when her Jeep disappeared down the road.

"There you are," his uncle called out after rushing to the side of his SUV. "When you get back, I want to see you and Amy in my office."

"Sure, what's up?" He frowned.

"Oh, nothing big, just wanted to run something by the pair of you." He glanced around the parking lot. "Did I miss Amy already?"

"Yeah, she just left. I'll text her you want to see us."

"Great." His uncle patted his hand and walked back into the building.

He'd been around the man for only a couple months, but already he felt closer to him than he had ever felt to his father. Which made him feel a pang of hurt in his chest every time he thought about it.

Growing up, he never really thought of his father as mean. Just strict. Sure, he was spanked with a belt until he couldn't sit straight, but what kid wasn't? Or so he'd thought his entire childhood.

Now, as an adult, he knew better and wished more than anything that his mother had left the bastard a long time ago. But he couldn't solely lay all the blame on her; after all, she got slapped around plenty back in those days too.

Now, his mother was set up in a nice condo in Cherry Creek and spent his dad's hard-earned pension while the bastard rotted in hell.

It had been nice to talk with Amy about his past, about his parents, and the way he'd been raised. She had given him pointers on how to deal with his mother, who was still in denial of the man's shortcomings as a father and husband. It was hard to be close to a woman who was still so forgiving of the man who had made Logan's childhood such a living hell.

He took a curve a little too fast and tried to clear his head from the unsettling thoughts, then purposely let his foot off the gas. He had plenty of time to get to his first appointment and didn't want to end up in a ditch somewhere. Especially since he had a few years left paying off the new car.

His mind played over his options as he slowly drove up the twisted road toward Black Hawk. Amy had kept all her listings in the Genesee area, while he'd started taking the farther ones in Black Hawk and Central City. The small towns had done a lot of booming since gambling was legalized over two decades ago.

Not only had he chosen the area because the roads were a lot more dangerous to drive in the winter, but because the class of the clientele was a lot different from those in the market for the much-higher-priced homes.

There were several developments going in that would house most of the employees and staff that worked in the big casinos. They still made quite a profit for RMR, which meant every buyer was treated equally.

He was early for his first appointment, so he let himself into the home and made sure the current owners had cleaned up as requested. He was thankful when he walked into the place and noticed it had been cleaned since the last showing he'd had a few days back.

When the potential buyers finally showed up, they argued the entire time he showed them the small place. She thought the home was perfect, while her husband or boyfriend thought the place was a pigsty. His words, not Logan's.

He doubted he'd hear anything more from the young couple and moved on to his next showing, an even smaller home right in downtown Central City. The place had been converted into a shop at one point and was commercially zoned.

His client, a young woman with jet-black hair and large green eyes, was already standing by the front door when he drove up.

"Hello," she almost whispered. "I'm Xina." Her voice was not only faint, but very eerie. "You should take the rest of the day off. Go see your loved ones," she said as she shook his hand.

His looked at her askance. "I'm sorry?"

"I'm sorry." She glanced toward the door. "Sometimes I ramble on." She motioned for him to show her around.

Less than ten minutes later, she took a deep breath. "The place is perfect for what I require." She stood just inside the front door. "The air in here is good and strong. I'll start my offer ten thousand lower than the asking price."

"Okay, if you'll give me a few minutes, I'll need a signature." He pulled out some paperwork and filled everything out quickly. He couldn't explain it, but the longer he was around her, the more eager he was to get away. "If you'll just sign here." She reached for the pen and her eyes met his.

"You'll need your keys. Don't forget your keys are in your back pocket," she said, then leaned down to sign the paperwork. "Thank you, Mr. Miller." She looked at him, and for a moment, he swore sadness crossed those green eyes of hers.

"Um, Miss . . ." He looked down at the paper for her name again.

"Xina. Just Xina." She didn't even turn back to him to answer.

"What is it you're using this shop for?" he asked.

"I'm a spiritual healer." She left as he felt a shiver run up his spine.

His next three listings weren't as exciting as the first two. The next woman he showed an apartment to instantly disliked the place. After that, he showed the same house from his first showing to another couple and they both seemed pleased and made an extremely low offer. The last one was to a single male who was looking at a higher-scale home on the outskirts of town up in the mountains.

The place was gorgeous. Five bedrooms, four and a half baths, with a built-in movie theater basement. He could just imagine himself with a man cave like that someday. Not to mention all those rooms for the kids he wanted. Every one of them looking a great deal like Amy.

He was on his way to his last meeting when Amy called. Pulling into a gas station, he answered, "Hey."

"Hi, are you about done?" She sounded winded.

"Yeah, are you okay?" He was instantly worried.

"Yes, the condo I just showed was on the fifth floor. I don't know why anyone would want to jog up five flights of stairs every day."

"Hey, my uncle wants to see us back at the office before we call it a weekend."

"Okay . . ." He could hear the question in her voice.

"I have no clue why. He said he just wanted to run something by us."

"Hmm. I'm heading back down now."

"I've got one last listing, then I'll be there." He glanced at his watch and calculated. "About an hour, if this appointment with these sellers goes fast."

"Okay, see you there." She made a kissing noise, which sent goose bumps all over his skin.

"I'll do that in person when I see you."

"Promise?" she whispered.

"Always." He smiled as she hung up.

He liked listing the higher-priced homes near Silver Gulch. The entire loop of homes ranged in the millions and were all under a year old. There was a private school, tennis courts, and if the rumors were true, a community swimming pool coming soon.

His appointment was with the current owners of the listing. He'd done his research on the home and hoped it was worthy of the price tag his clients had placed on it. The man who'd insisted on being the last appointment of the day had sounded eager to sell.

As Logan drove up the private drive, he whistled.

The place was bigger than the home he and Amy had shown the Penningtons. He frowned when he noticed that part of the giant place was still under construction. Parking his car, he got out, tucked his keys into his pocket and reached for his bag.

◆ ◆ ◆

When Amy got back to the office, she handed the single offer she'd received to one of the other agents to type up and send out the next morning. She chatted with the office rats, what everyone called all the wannabe-Realtors who did the filing and paperwork. Then she headed back to her desk and took her time answering a pile of emails she'd been putting off.

After she was done, she glanced at the clock. Walking down the long hallway, she peeked her head into Gary's office.

"Is Logan back yet?" she asked.

Gary looked up from his computer, a pair of black bifocals hanging on the edge of his nose.

"Not yet." He looked down at his watch. "Should be back any minute."

She pulled out her cell phone. She hated to call him if he was with a client, or driving down a windy mountain road. Tapping her phone to her chin she decided to wait a few more minutes.

"Why don't you come in here and wait? I'm sure he's just stuck with a client."

She nodded and walked over to sit in one of two soft leather chairs.

"So, any hint as to what you want to talk to us about?" She smiled as she tried to hide her nerves. She knew everything was going great at the agency, and to be honest, had hoped it had something to do with a promotion. But she doubted he'd bring both Logan and her in as partners. The issue had her torn: she wanted the promotion, but was still uncertain about how she felt regarding Logan's place in the firm.

Over the last two months, he'd proven to her that he was just as hard a worker as she was. He was smart, loyal, and . . . she was about to add the word *sexy* to her list. Giggling to herself, she blinked and waited for Gary to set his glasses down and look at her.

"Nope, not until Logan gets here." He leaned back in his chair. "So, tell me how it's been going."

She sighed because she hated small talk with Gary. He somehow always made it seem like a counseling session instead of friendly conversation.

She talked about her listings for the week and slowly watched the time tick by. When fifteen minutes had passed, she pulled out her phone and typed a quick text message to Logan.

Where r u?

When she didn't get a response, her foot started tapping on the floor. She tried again five minutes later. After five more, she dialed his number. When it went to his voice mail, she jumped up to ask Ana where his last appointment was.

Ana mentioned a client's name, but no address.

"Why don't we check his computer?" Gary suggested over her shoulder.

She raced down the hall and logged into his machine.

Scribbling down the address, she picked up the phone and dialed Central City's police—only for the police operator to tell her that address wasn't valid.

"What do you mean it's not valid? I'm looking at an MLS of the property right now," she insisted into the phone.

"I'm sorry, but it's not in our system yet. If it's a new home . . ."

She glanced quickly over the paper. "Yes, it is. Can you send someone out there? The nearest intersection is . . ." She rattled off the street names and felt her heart jump faster.

"I'll see what we can do. There's a convention in town and most of our troopers are busy with that."

Shutting off her phone, she looked over at Gary, who had turned a deep shade of red.

"Get your keys. We're going for a drive." Then he pointed to Ana, who was crowding in the doorway with a few other people. "Don't leave until he comes back and give us a call the second he does, if he does."

She nodded as Amy dragged him out the door. Worry was begging to win out in her mind and she was starting to feel a little lightheaded at the thought of something terrible happening to Logan.

A ton of reasons as to why he hadn't checked in or answered his phone popped into her mind. He could have car problems. He could have gotten lost on a side road and didn't have cell service. A tree could have fallen on his car, trapping him as a hungry bear slowly crept— She shook her head and tried to stop all the nonsense from flooding her thoughts as she drove up the mountains with his uncle sitting beside her.

CHAPTER
NINETEEN

Logan tried to open his eyes, but instantly felt pain shooting through his temple. Groaning, he tried to reach up and touch the spot only to realize his hands were secured behind his back.

Shaking his head, he smelled dirt and blood. The mixture sent shock waves through him. The room was too dark for him to see clearly, not to mention his head was killing him, causing his eyes to blur.

He was lying on the ground. He could see a faint light from one corner and rolled his body until he sat on his knees. When a wave of dizziness hit him, he shook his head lightly and took several deep breaths.

Then he remembered what had happened. Or what he assumed had happened. He hadn't seen who had hit him and could only guess that whoever it had been had stolen his car and all of his belongings.

Panic set in when he realized he was in an unfinished basement. It was massive. The room was easily bigger than Amy's entire townhouse and his apartment together.

Looking around again, he tried to find something to break his arms free. But so far there was only dirt and ceiling. There weren't even windows, which had him looking back toward the faint light in shock.

Terror overcame him as he saw that the small spot had grown and was now a deep red. Flames were now visible, and he could see smoke billowing around that section of ceiling.

Taking a few deep breaths, he patted his pocket and groaned when he realized he'd left his cell phone in the middle console of his car after the call from Amy.

He rolled onto his back and tried to stand up, only to have something jab him.

"You'll need your keys. Don't forget your keys are in your back pocket." He heard Xina's voice in his head.

Rolling again, he twisted until he felt the bulge of his keys in his back pocket. Whoever had jumped him hadn't taken his car keys after all. Carefully taking them out, he used his car key to work on the duct tape that held his hands secure.

♦ ♦ ♦

"So far he hasn't checked in with the office." Gary shut off his phone as Amy concentrated on the road. "They haven't heard from him and he still isn't answering his phone." He slammed the End button and growled, "They got word from the clients that the road had been blocked and they had assumed the meeting was canceled."

"I'm sure he's just out of the service area. This is a new construction area above Black Hawk. Maybe they haven't put in towers yet?" She kept trying to convince herself.

They were less than five minutes away when she realized that this is probably how Logan had felt that day the Jeep wouldn't start. Chuckling to herself, she glanced over at Gary, who was looking at her like she was crazy.

At the moment, she did feel crazy. Panic had consumed her mind since they'd left the office. Just the thought of never seeing Logan again had her eyes burning and her chest tightening. She'd never felt like this about a man before. Then realization dawned on her and she felt her heart skip.

"I love him," she said out loud.

Gary blinked a few times and then laughed. "Hell, everyone in the office knows that, dear."

"Well, someone should have told me then." She felt her shoulders start to relax.

"I'm sure you're right. He probably just has no reception. After all, the house looks huge."

She chanced a glance down at the paperwork he held. "Yeah, easily seven thousand square feet."

When they took the turnoff that led to the mountain, they saw the blockade the clients had talked about.

"Stay here. I'll see what's up," Gary said, getting out of the car.

She watched him approach the barricades. There weren't any police officers around, or for that matter, any other cars. So, after he looked around, he pushed the barricade aside and motioned for her to drive through.

"Are you going to put it back?" she asked when he got back in the Jeep.

"No, I have a bad feeling about this." He frowned over at her as he picked up his phone. "Maybe you'd better step on it while I call the police."

◆　◆　◆

Logan felt his wrists bleeding from the constant back and forth motion, but he kept on using his keys to cut through layer after layer of duct tape. Whoever had secured him didn't want him to get loose.

His eyes kept traveling back to the flames. He'd even taken time out from cutting to roll to the other side of the basement, which was no more than a crawl-space size.

Finally, he felt the tape start to give way and wrenched his hands several times until they broke free.

Tucking his keys back in his pocket, he glanced around and wondered what was next. Since there weren't any windows, he had to find another way out. Surely whoever had put him here had used a door. He looked back to where he'd been lying when he woke and saw a sliver of light above the spot.

As he rushed over, he felt panic hit as the flames licked above his head. Gone, his only exit route was gone. He rushed back to his safe corner and huddled down trying to think of another way out.

Images of Amy flooded his mind. He'd been cheated out of telling her exactly how he felt. And of the family he'd dreamed of having with her. Even seeing Daisy's puppies grow up.

Tears stung his eyes as smoke flooded the area.

"You'll need your keys. Don't forget your keys are in your back pocket." Xina's voice sounded again in his head.

"Yeah, what good are these going to do me now?" He looked down at them. Taking a chance, he hit the alarm button on the key and heard his car alarm start to squawk.

◆ ◆ ◆

Gary hung up the phone with the police the second the Jeep turned the last corner and they saw the bright orange of the flames ahead. Then she heard him talking to the fire department.

Amy's heart fell and she felt a wave of panic overtake her. The Jeep's tires threw up gravel as they stopped right beside Logan's SUV.

"Logan!" Gary and she jumped out of the Jeep and started yelling at the same time.

"You go that way." Gary pointed to the left. "Don't go running in there. It's too far gone at this point."

She nodded and ran to the left. They sprinted around the entire building, screaming his name and listening for any sounds. When they finally made it back to the Jeep, the fire truck was coming up the drive.

The house was sixty percent gone by the time they hooked up their hoses.

"Please," she cried, watching the flames. "Please just give us a sign he's okay." She couldn't get her eyes to look away from the building.

"Is anyone inside?" A fireman rushed over to them and pulled them both back a few steps.

"Logan," she whispered.

"We think my nephew is in there," Gary said in a stressed voice.

"Any idea where?" the fireman asked.

They both shook their heads, then jumped when his car alarm started going off. Then it beeped secure, then back to the alarm. This happened five times. Then it dawned on her that Logan must be doing it.

"He's in there. He's alive," she cried as the fireman and Gary held her back. "Help him!"

The fireman rushed away.

"There! He's got to be close to the car. I've got the same model and the damn key won't work unless I'm within ten feet," a different fireman said, pointing to the corner of the house. He pushed past them with a hose in his hands.

For the next ten minutes, they fought the flames back from the corner of the house that wasn't yet burning. Firemen entered the main floor of the building only to come back out the windows empty-handed.

"He's not in here," he said over the alarm that kept turning on and off again.

"He has to be," she cried, just as the floor on the other side of the building collapsed and sank into the ground.

"The basement!" someone screamed. "Cut through the floor."

♦　♦　♦

Logan was getting tired. He huddled in the dark corner in the dirt with his jacket over his mouth and nose as he continued to hit his alarm. He prayed that someone was out there, trying to help him. At one point, he thought there was water spraying on his head, but shook the thought off, believing it had been just his imagination when he reached up and touched his dry hair.

He was getting faint from the lack of oxygen, so he lay down in the dirt and wedged himself between the cool earth and the concrete wall. His mind kept playing over images from his dreams as he continued to set off his car alarm.

In his mind he saw Amy walking down a long church aisle in a flowing white dress. Her long hair was pinned up, diamonds sparkled around her face. Then the scene flashed to a home in the hills. Daisy and her puppies ran free in a large green backyard. There was a swing set and Amy was pushing a little girl on a swing while a boy chased the dogs around.

Then he felt Amy hovering over him, her hair framing her face as she looked down at him.

"Wake up, Logan. Please," she begged him over and over again. "Don't leave me." He felt her tears running down his cheek. But when he raised his hands to wipe them from her eyes, his body wouldn't move. Instead, his hands were tied behind his back again as flames crept closer and closer.

♦　♦　♦

"Here!" someone shouted. "They have him."

Amy's attention moved over to where two men were pulling a very limp black mass from the basement. The firemen had broken through to the basement by cutting into the floor above and dropping a ladder down. She'd never seen firemen work before, but had instantly been impressed that four men had forsaken their own safety and climbed into the heart of a fire for a stranger.

"He's not breathing," someone yelled as they carried Logan toward the ambulance, which had parked directly behind her Jeep.

Gary and she were beside the gurney on which they laid him down. They stood back as a fireman tossed off his gloves and hat and started CPR on Logan immediately. Amy's heart felt like it had stopped as she watched the man kneeling over Logan and pounding against his chest. Every time they pumped oxygen into him, she held her breath. She couldn't look away as the EMTs continued to pump oxygen into his lungs.

Quickly, her mind flashed to a future without Logan. She physically felt her heart hurt as she thought of it. Her stomach rolled and she tried to focus on what was going on instead of the horror of possibilities.

Since the driveway was gravel, they had a hard time moving the gurney back toward the ambulance and the fireman actually had to get off and help carry it toward the vehicle.

"I'm going with them," she told Gary. "Here." She shoved her keys into his hands. "Follow us."

Tears were streaming down his face, and he used his sleeves to wipe them away. "I'll call his mother."

She jumped into the back of the ambulance as they continued to pump oxygen into Logan's lifeless body.

CHAPTER
TWENTY

Logan was drifting. This was a hell of a lot more peaceful than dying in a fire, he thought, which only shook him out of the surreal mindset. The word *fire* flashed memories into his brain as he screamed to his body to wake up. Amy!

His eyes opened slowly. His entire body felt like he'd jogged a thousand miles. His lungs burned when he tried to take a deep breath.

"No, don't move." He heard Amy, and blinked frantically, desperate to see her. "You're safe." He couldn't see her, but heard the relief in her voice. "We're at St. Anthony's." He felt her take his hand and tried to open his eyes again. "Easy, don't worry. Give your eyes some time. They say there's a lot of smoke and dirt in them still."

He continued to blink, but so far his vision was still too fuzzy to make anything out clearly. Then he tried to open his mouth.

"No." She brought his hand up to her face and he felt a tear fall down her cheek. "They don't want you to speak either. I guess for the next few days you're going to have to let me do all the talking."

He nodded slowly and swallowed.

"They don't want you to have any water just yet." He knew her voice well and he could tell that she'd been very worried. She sounded as if she hadn't slept for days. "I know you probably want some, but you'll have to hang on." She brushed at his hair and she sat next to him on the bed.

He nodded slightly, enjoying the touch of her fingers on his skin.

"They're looking for whoever tied you up and did this to you." He felt her touch the bruised spot on the side of his head lightly. He remembered the pain and the blood then. Reaching up with his free hand, he took hers and squeezed. Then brought it to his lips and left it there until he heard her sob.

"It's okay. I'm okay," he tried to say, but it came out only as a croak.

Then she rested her head on his shoulder. "I'm in love with you," she cried out against his chest. "Don't you ever leave me," she sobbed.

He shook his head and held her close, running his fingers through her hair. He couldn't stop the tears from falling down his cheeks as he held her. Now, when he needed his voice the most, it was gone. Once he opened his eyes, he realized the tears had cleared the smoke from them and he was able to see a little better. Still, everything had a hazy film and he blinked a few more times to try to focus more.

"Oh," he heard a new voice. "How wonderful." He smiled when he looked over and recognized his mother's shape. Holding out his hand, he motioned for her to come closer.

He watched a dark gray blob move toward him, and when he felt his mother's hand in his, he tugged Amy's up to meet hers. "I guess this is his way of introducing us." He smiled when Amy started nervously twisting her watch.

"Well, dear, I already know who you are of course." He could tell that Amy had crossed the room and assumed the two women were hugging. "Logan used to be such a pain to you. Wasn't he?"

He heard Amy chuckle and he felt his cheeks go hot.

"There you are, boy!" His uncle burst into the conversation. He didn't know if the man had stood back and watched the last few minutes or if he'd just stepped into the room. Either way, it was perfect timing. "You know, there are better ways to get out of a meeting with me than this." His uncle laughed at his own joke.

Logan just shook his head and motioned for him to spill it.

"What? What's that, my boy?"

"I think he wants to know what your meeting was about," Amy said. Logan nodded his head a few times.

His uncle laughed. "Well, you'll just have to get better to find out. Won't you?"

Amy groaned, and Logan would have, too, if he could have.

"They want to keep him for a few days. Until he's back to his old self." He heard Amy tell the room, but he couldn't see her face clearly to tell if she was hiding something.

He held out his hand until she took it. Then he squeezed.

"Really, they just want to make sure your eyes are okay." He tilted his head. "Okay, they're really worried about your head." She sighed. "You stopped breathing for over ten minutes." He heard her sob. "The fireman who pulled you out of the house pounded on your chest until we were halfway down the mountain."

He tugged on her hand until she laid her head on his chest. He heard his mother crying and hoped his uncle was comforting her.

"There, there," his uncle finally said, sniffling. "He's awake now. No use crying about what might have been."

He smiled when Amy used a tissue to softly dry his own tears. He blinked a few times and could see a little more clearly to make out the outline of her face.

"Beautiful." It came out as a whisper as his fingers brushed against her soft skin.

"Logan!" she exclaimed. "You're not supposed to talk."

Just the sound of her voice was doing more than any rest could do to his system. Having her beside him was the best medicine he could ever get.

"I love you," he said hoarsely. He'd pay the price for those three words later as he felt flames shoot up his throat.

His vision cleared further, and he watched tears start to flood her beautiful eyes as she bit her bottom lip. As her eyes moved to his, her lips turned upward into a smile.

"I love you too." She laughed. "Now shut up." She hugged him and he felt her body shake. He held onto her until he heard his mother and uncle leave the room quietly.

His heart was beating fast as she placed soft kisses along his chin. He'd never imagined that he could have gotten so lucky.

♦ ♦ ♦

The next day, Amy was still in Logan's room when they were visited by a state investigator who, at this point, had more questions than answers about what had happened. In the end, she had stood her ground and asked the man to leave because Logan couldn't use his voice yet.

So far, Amy had left his side only to rush home to shower and change. She'd persuaded Kristen to stay at her place see to the dogs' needs until Logan was out of the hospital.

The day before he was set to be released, three crime-scene investigators knocked on his door.

"Mr. Miller." The oldest of the group was a silver-haired man who looked to be in his early fifties. "I'm Carl Wither, I'm an arson inspector for McWilliams Insurance. These gentlemen are from the state and county."

Logan nodded and shook all three men's hands. The men sat down and explained how the owner of the construction company that had built the home had been caught trying to get into Canada with his wife. They had over a million dollars taped to their bodies. Apparently, they had been using the homeowner's money to gamble instead of using it to finish the house. The investigators had proof that the pair had lost big at the casino a few weeks ago and had withdrawn the remaining cash.

"The fire initially looked legit," Mr. Wither said. "It started at the fuse box and spread without help. That is, if you don't count the cheap material that they used in the home. The only thing that tipped us off that it could be arson was you . . . what happened to you," he corrected.

"Why . . . ?" he started to ask, but Amy jumped in.

"Why did they attack Logan?" She squeezed his hand, not wanting him to use his voice too much.

"They claimed that they didn't know the owner had scheduled an appointment with Mr. Miller. They never even imagined that the owner would try to sell the house, since construction wasn't completed yet," one of the other men said.

"Why did they attack him?" she persisted.

Mr. Wither jumped in. "We're not too sure on why. Maybe they saw him drive up as they were starting the fire and panicked?" The older man ran his hands through his hair. "Either way, they'll be charged with attempted murder as well as fraud and a long list of other things."

"Why didn't the owners . . . ?" His voice cracked and he swallowed. Amy quickly handed him some water.

Mr. Wither nodded. "I think you're asking why they weren't there to meet you." Logan nodded after taking a sip. "It seems like your clients were running very late, and by the time they made it to the street, the blockade your uncle and Miss Walker here moved aside did the trick for them." He glanced at Amy. "They turned around thinking the road was closed. They claimed it's been closed several times before and they had been told never to drive through if it was blocked. Later that evening, after they had made it back into town, they had called your office to make sure the meeting had been canceled."

After the men left his room, Amy crawled into his bed with him and enjoyed having him hold her. Her mind kept playing over and over how close she'd come to losing him.

She'd been so close to never knowing how wonderful it felt to know she wanted to spend the rest of her life with him. She still worried about marriage, but with Logan, she knew they would be able to overcome anything together.

◆ ◆ ◆

In the end, they kept Logan in the hospital for five days, until he had his full eyesight and voice back. He had seven stitches above his left ear, and since they had to shave that part of his head, he had a stylish new 'do that his friends playfully ridiculed.

Gary wouldn't let Logan or Amy come back to work that first week, but she had promised to bring him into the office so he could see everyone. He'd told her that he wanted to let everyone see firsthand that he was alive and well.

Aiden and Gary had spent a whole day moving all of Logan's things into her townhouse. She'd been secretly looking for a bigger place, since the puppies were up and running around. They needed a backyard to play in, not the small piece of grass she currently had.

She loved having him live with her, even the dogs seemed much happier. They both enjoyed spending as much time with the dogs as they could while Logan recovered. She knew that their time off from work was coming to an end. Logan was almost back to his old self. They were both feeling antsy and ready to get to work again.

An hour into their first day, Gary walked into their office with a huge pair of scissors.

"What the heck do you need those for?" Logan joked as he leaned slightly in his chair.

"If you two are done with your vacation, follow me." He turned and walked out of the office.

"Vacation?" Logan took Amy's hand and followed him to the elevator.

"What's this about?" Logan asked when the elevator started to move.

"You'll see." Gary chuckled.

When the elevator doors opened, there was a bright red ribbon blocking their path. Everyone from the office stood on the other side, smiling at them.

"Now, if you'd do the honors." Gary handed the scissors to Logan. Logan looked down at them, then over at her. "Together?" He smiled. She nodded and took his hand and helped him cut the ribbon.

"It's official. The executive suite of Rocky Mountain Realty is now open for business. And as one the three owners, I'd like to introduce you to the other two." He raised his arms and stepped to the side. "The soon to be Mr. and Mrs. Logan Miller."

Everyone clapped and cheered as Logan pulled her into his arms and kissed her right in front of everyone. Then he moved back. "Easy, darling." He took a few mock deep breaths. "I did almost suffocate a couple weeks ago."

"How can I ever forget?" She wrapped one arm around him, never wanting to let go.

◆ ◆ ◆

Amy took a deep breath and rolled her shoulders. It was now or never. She turned and smiled at Kristen, who looked absolutely stunning in her dress and veil.

"Ready?" Amy whispered.

"It's now or never," Kristen said.

Amy chuckled. "My thinking exactly. Good luck."

Kristen smiled to her friend, then Amy turned and started walking slowly up the church aisle, smiling at everyone she knew as she passed them in the pews. She'd been avoiding making eye contact with Logan since she'd walked into the church. But as she stopped in front, her eyes moved to his and she felt her knees go a little weak. Which was the reason she'd avoided eye contact in the first place.

Taking a few deep breaths, she looked to the back of the church when the music changed and felt tears sting her eyes as Kristen started walking down the aisle on her father's arm.

Glancing over, she watched Aiden's expression and felt a tear escape when she noticed his wet eyes. How could she have known there was so much love out there? Her eyes moved to the right side, to where her parents sat, holding hands, and Amy felt like laughing.

She would have never imagined in a million years that their relationship would have worked the way that it did. That because of a stupid piece of paper and vows said in front of loved ones, they couldn't make it work together. But take all that away and they were perfect for each other.

Glancing once more at Logan, she felt her heart flutter knowing that it didn't matter if there was a piece of paper, or a building on fire, she would love this man until her dying breath. No matter what.

She stood in front of the church and listened to her best friend read her own vows. By the time Aiden was done with his, there wasn't a dry eye in the church. Then everyone laughed as Kristen stumbled when the priest told Aiden he could kiss his bride. She'd tripped right into his arms and he didn't waste a single moment as he planted his lips over hers and everyone cheered.

The reception was held a few doors down at the historic Golden Hotel. The entire ballroom was decked out, thanks to the best bridesmaids a girl could ever have.

The dance floor was crowded as everyone enjoyed their time into the night. The food was delicious, the cake beautiful, and the mood was so romantic, Amy doubted anything could have been more perfect.

When Logan pulled her onto the dance floor, she was a little shocked that no one else was dancing, then the room went silent as a spotlight shone down on them.

"Amy, I've been wanting to do this since the first time I said 'I love you' . . ." The entire room *aahed* in unison. "So, Aiden and Kristen graciously allowed me a moment in the spotlight." He glanced up as everyone chuckled. Then they went silent again as he bent down on one knee and pulled a small black box from his jacket pocket.

"Amy Walker, I'd go through heaven and hell to be with you. I want to grow old and raise puppies and kids with you. With you next to me, I'd be the luckiest man alive. Will you marry me?"

She wiped the tears from her eyes and nodded. "Yes, of course I will."

ABOUT THE AUTHOR

Photo © 2015 Daryl Sanders

Jill Sanders is *The New York Times* and *USA Today* bestselling author of the Pride Series, Secret Series, West, and Grayton Series romance novels. She continues to lure new readers with her sweet and sexy stories. Her books are available in every English-speaking country as audiobooks, and are now being translated into six different languages.

Born as an identical twin to a large family, she was raised in the Pacific Northwest, later relocating to Colorado for college and a successful IT career before discovering her talent as a writer. She now makes her home along the Emerald Coast in Florida where she enjoys the beach, hiking, swimming, wine tasting, and of course writing. Readers can connect with Jill on Facebook (www.facebook.com/JillSandersBooks) and Twitter (@JillMSanders) or visit her website, www.JillSanders.com.